Gods and

Book 1 of Dark Streets

By BR Kingsolver

Cover art by Heather Hamilton-Senter

http://www.bookcoverartistry.com/

Cover model from Cover Stock Photos

http://coverstockphotos.com/

Copyright 2018

~ ~ ~

License Notes

Other books by BR Kingsolver

The Chameleon Assassin Series
Chameleon Assassin
Chameleon Uncovered
Chameleon's Challenge
Chameleon's Death Dance

The Telepathic Clans Saga
The Succubus Gift
Succubus Unleashed
Broken Dolls
Succubus Rising
Succubus Ascendant

Other books
I'll Sing for my Dinner
Trust

Short Stories in Anthologies
Here, Kitty Kitty
Bellator

BRKingsolver.com
Facebook
Twitter

Table of Contents

Chapter 1 1

Chapter 2 11

Chapter 3 22

Chapter 4 33

Chapter 5 40

Chapter 6 53

Chapter 7 60

Chapter 8 70

Chapter 9 83

Chapter 10 92

Chapter 11 102

Chapter 12 111

Chapter 13 123

Chapter 14 130

Chapter 15 137

Chapter 16 143

Chapter 17 154

Chapter 18 161

Chapter 19 169

Chapter 20 176

Chapter 21 184

Chapter 22 190

Chapter 23 197

Chapter 24 205

Chapter 25 214

Chapter 26 224

Chapter 27 231

Chapter 28 240

Chapter 29 247

Gods and Demons

CHAPTER 1

A woman walking home late at night has a choice. She can either walk in the light and hope people will help her if she has any trouble, or she can walk in the shadows and hope no one sees her. I figured no woman in her right mind walked through dark streets at night, so the predators should be looking elsewhere.

Of course, it didn't require an IQ test to become a criminal, or a rogue Werewolf with robbery or rape on his mind. Maybe I needed to reevaluate my state of mind and my decision-making processes.

Three Werewolves in their Human forms stepped out of the shadows. A quick glance over my shoulder showed two more behind me. Under the circumstances, I didn't think their intentions were honorable.

My sword whispered out of its sheath almost soundlessly, but I was sure the Weres heard it. I didn't think I could take five Weres with only a sword, but mostly I hoped it would distract them. I surreptitiously sketched a rune with my other hand and spoke a Word under my breath.

A wild animal roared, filling the alley with a heart-stopping sound, and then the world caved in on the Weres standing in front of me. A dark shape fell from a roof to my right, landing on two of the Weres and knocking the third one against the far wall.

The shape resolved itself as an animal of some sort, maybe a large cat. Definitely a cat. It clawed the two men with all four feet. It bit one of the Weres in the head. I heard bones crunch and he went limp. The third man moved toward it with something in his hand. The cat slapped him. His head swiveled on his neck, and I noted that as he fell, his face continued to look over his shoulder. The cat bit the second Were's head and then turned to look at me.

The entire fight took only a few seconds. I shook myself out of my shock and spun to face the Weres behind me. They stood frozen, but I guess my movement caught their attention. Proving they weren't complete fools, both turned and ran. I was tempted to send the spell I held after them, but I knew I wasn't alone in the alley.

I turned back and discovered the cat was gone.

A woman walked toward me. She stood no taller than my chest and appeared to be a full-figured Mexican peasant woman—similar to many of the hotel maids in the city—dressed in blue jeans, a loose white blouse, and a khaki jacket. She had dark skin, a Mayan nose, and her dark hair hung down her back in a braid as thick as my wrist. I shouldn't have been able to see her eyes in the dark, but a thin ring of yellow surrounded her dilated pupils.

"Didn't your mama tell you not to walk down dark alleys at night?" she asked in a Spanish accent.

"My mother said a lot of things I should probably have paid attention to." I realized that I had seen her before—just an hour earlier at the club where I was listening to an Irish band—she had brushed against me at the bar when I was getting another beer.

She chuckled. "Perhaps we should find somewhere else to talk," she said. "Before anyone decides to ask questions."

Without another word, she turned and started

walking down the alley, stepping over and around the bodies of the Weres she had killed. I sheathed my sword and followed her. I wasn't sure the sword would help me against a being that could turn three muggers into Werewolf tartare without breaking a sweat. Two of the Weres were shredded, soaked in blood, and their skulls were crushed. The third guy had a broken neck, and the side of his head and face were marked by four bone-deep slashes.

Whatever my mysterious benefactor was, she was absolutely the baddest woman I had ever met. I hoped that I would wake up in the morning and discover she was only part of a weird dream. Or maybe she wasn't some kind of shifter. Maybe she was a mage and she'd called a demon or something. That thought didn't make me feel any better.

"Where are you going?" she asked.

"Home."

"Okay. We need to talk."

I stopped. The last thing I wanted to do was go anywhere with her. The whole scene in the alley was a horror show, and I just wanted to get as far away from it, and her, as I could. After a few steps, she realized I wasn't with her and turned. I tried to keep my hand from shaking as I held out my business card.

"It's late, and I'm beat," I said. "Come by my office in the morning."

She took the card and nodded. "All right. Try to stay out of dark alleys. *Buenas noches.*"

I watched her walk away. She moved silently and with a sinuous grace that didn't seem to fit her build. I released the spell I had been holding. Whether it would have stopped her—or her familiar—was something I wasn't eager to test.

3

Not wanting to be followed to my house, I went to work rather than go home. I had a small cottage on the property where I lived when I first started the business. There was no chance of anyone invading it.

The cottage was a bit rustic and cramped with only three rooms. I built it when I first bought the land, as I didn't have any money to rent an apartment. It didn't even have heat or electricity the first few years, I just spelled light and heat.

My landscaping business covered eighteen acres of prime real estate near American University. I couldn't afford such land at current prices, as evidenced by some of the eye-popping offers I had recently received, but it was fairly cheap when I bought it forty-five years before. There wasn't any way I could find enough land for a nursery close to DC if I sold it.

As I walked past one of the four oaks that anchored the corners of the property, a Fairy swooped down and landed on my shoulder. She chattered in my ear, mostly about a neighbor's dog, while I unlocked the gate and let myself in. I hoped that my Fairy nest buried the evidence if they decided to deal with the offending animal.

Fred and Kate, my garden Gnomes, had already gone to bed, and no light shone from the windows of their mound. When I entered the cottage, it smelled a little musty, and I opened a couple of windows to let it air out. I hadn't stayed there in a while. After a quick shower, I snuggled under the covers in a bed that felt comfortingly familiar.

My crews showed up at six in the morning. I didn't need to get up, but I rolled out of bed anyway.

Looking out the window, I saw that my foreman, Ed Gillespie, had everything under control. He handed out work orders, helped the crews load up the plants and the equipment each would need, and sent them out the gate.

After a quick shower, I showed up with a cup of tea and watched.

"Hey, sleepy head," Ed called. "Late night and didn't make it home? Did ya get any?"

Various crewmembers called out greetings. The feeling was familiar and comfortable, and I needed it after the horror of the night before. I realized that I must have been in shock after witnessing that slaughter. It was a wonder I didn't run screaming from whatever it was that wore the form of a woman.

For forty years I had done all the mind-numbing paperwork, accounting, phone calls, and routine work. I was glad to pass as much of it as I could to Maurine, my office manager, Kathy, my accountant, and Ed. I still had to sign the checks and contracts and other things.

I was finishing up the morning's necessary paperwork and had almost forgotten the previous night's events when the woman from the alley walked through my office door at nine o'clock. She sat in one of the chairs in front of my desk and looked around. I judged her to be older than I originally thought. Somewhere in her forties, maybe.

"Nice place. Landscape architect. Makes sense. You don't look any the worse for wear from last night," she said.

"I didn't do anything last night. Look, I'm grateful for your help, but I don't get involved with the paranormal community. I just happened to be in the wrong place at the wrong time."

"Ah, well, then I'll state my business quickly," she said. "I need an Elf, or a very strong witch with very specialized skills. An Elf would be better, especially a realm walker."

I didn't bother to ask why she was talking to me about Elves, but rather stared at her. My shock from the night before returned, and I felt numb.

"Kellana Rogirsdottir," the woman said, reading my card that she held. "Sounds almost Icelandic." She turned her face up to me. "What is it really?"

"Kellana ap th'Rogir," I said.

"And you're from Alfheim?"

"Midgard." I tried to shake myself out of my daze. "I'm not a realm walker."

"Oh? And how did you get here?"

I felt almost hypnotized, staring into her yellow eyes.

"I came here with a realm walker," I said. "A less than honorable man." Why did I say that last part? She had me completely unsettled.

She raised an eyebrow. "And he abandoned you here?"

"After a manner of speaking. He died."

Alaric was handsome, exciting, and full of wild ideas and promises. He decided that we should come to Earth, a realm with little magic, and get rich. Realm walkers were the most successful thieves imaginable. I was young and dumb, and although his plan made me uncomfortable, his kisses and his hands drove me wild and jumbled any thoughts in my silly head.

He walked us into the realm of Earth at a place called Dresden on February 14, 1945. If he hadn't been standing in front of me, the bomb would have killed me, too. When I picked myself up, I found I had come to the place Humans called Hell.

I shook myself out of my reverie. "I don't think I can help you."

She breathed a deep sigh. "I am looking for an artifact. A portal. I know who had it, and I followed him here to Washington. But he's dead, and he didn't have the artifact when I found his body."

"I still don't understand how you think I can help, Miss..."

"Isabella Cortez. Doctor Isabella Cortez. I can't feel the artifact, Sel Kellana. You see, I don't have any magic. An Elf could detect it, I hope, as could certain types of witches or mages. Human mages might feel it, but I think a mage from another realm might have better luck."

I shrugged. "An artifact that's a portal? I don't think I've ever heard of such a thing, and I'm not a mage." I stood. "I wish you luck, Dr. Cortez. Thank you for last night, but I have work to do."

I thought she was going to be difficult, but she shook my hand, gave me her business card, and graciously departed. My talents didn't include precognition, but it didn't take a soothsayer for me to suspect I hadn't seen the last of her. It was only after she left that I wondered how she knew I was an Elf and knew enough about Elves to use the 'Sel' honorific in addressing me.

Of course, for so many years Humans considered the possibility of other races as fantasies. Lately, they were more apt to wonder about my humanity.

My afternoon appointment in Chevy Chase involved the type of work I enjoyed. A couple had recently bought a house. As was often the case, the lawns and garden had once been nice, but age and neglect had left them in a pitiful state. The woman I met with wanted a showplace, a beautiful garden to match her large, fancy house.

I soon learned that she wasn't a gardener and wanted the landscaping only to look at. She had no intention of ever getting her hands dirty by taking care of it. So, I needed to come up with an eye-popping design with some unusual elements to wow her friends, and an on-going maintenance contract to keep my crews busy. I heard the cash register in my head ring repeatedly as I walked around the place, sketching and taking notes.

After promising that I would have a design for her the following week, I got in my pickup and backed out of her driveway. No traffic, just a car parked down the street. Glancing in my rearview mirror while I drove off, I saw the car pull away from the curb and follow me. I didn't think anything about it until I was about halfway back to the nursery. The car was still following me.

I drove into a fast-food place and bought a milkshake. When I pulled out again, the car soon reappeared behind me. Since I led a fairly low-key lifestyle, and no one knew I was an Elf, such an occurrence was unusual.

The type of run-in I had the previous night was rare, though more common the past couple of years. Two years before, on Beltane when the veils between realms were thinnest, celestial alignments led to the veils thinning to the point of rupture. Rumor was that Vampires hired a demon to actually cause the rupture, but other rumors said Werewolves hired a realm walker.

No matter the cause, creatures from other realms flooded into Earth's realm, including thousands of Vampires and Weres. Demons rampaged on the

Capitol Mall, and even invaded the halls of Congress. Werewolves created a crisis in London.

Humanity's long denial of the supernatural shattered overnight. The Chinese used nuclear weapons against an invasion of demons and shredded the veils. Even beings without magic walked between realms, and two years later, the veils remained fragile.

As the awareness of paranormal beings and witchcraft spread, rioting broke out in many places. Witches, or suspected witches, and other non-Humans were persecuted and murdered in many places. The magic users and non-Humans fought back. Martial law was declared in all or part of seven southern states in the U.S., and China reverted to savage barbarism in an ongoing war against demons.

In other places, mages and witches began practicing magic publicly, Vampires opened nightclubs to prey on starry-eyed college girls, and TV reality shows became circus-like extravaganzas.

When Samhain came six months later, it became evident that Earth wasn't the only realm affected. All the realms descended into chaos. Enough Elves—refugees from strife in Alfheim and Midgard—settled in Iceland to start their own political party. I had met two other Elves in my first seventy years on Earth, but suddenly there were thousands of us living openly throughout the world.

But having two men in a black Mercedes follow me around was a first.

Since I was driving a pickup truck with my business logo that said, "Fairyland Landscape Design and Maintenance" on the doors and tailgate, it seemed silly to try and lose them, so I drove back to the nursery.

Driving through the gate, I saw the Fairies out

among the flowerbeds, and that made me think of Isabella Cortez. Any non-Humans entering my land would draw the Fairies out in full battle mode to defend their territory, but Cortez didn't attract their notice. Very curious.

My followers didn't try to enter after me but drove on past.

CHAPTER 2

I considered spending another night at the cottage, but I didn't have any clothes or food there. Making a note to remedy those things, I decided to brave the wild streets of Washington and go home. The wards on my house in Georgetown were as strong as the ones on the nursery, though they weren't anchored by the oak trees, and the house didn't have the Fairies for watchmen.

After dark settled, I jumped over the fence into the park that bordered my land on the opposite side from the gate into the nursery. Wearing a black ankle-length cloak with a hood, and using a glamour to blur my image, I checked around the corner. The Mercedes was still there.

All Elves had the ability to shrink to a more fae-like size, but rarely used it. My teachers said it was a vestigial evolutionary trait. Some said the Elves had once been only as small as the rest of the fae. No one had ever answered me when I asked if we had wings then.

I didn't want the men in the Mercedes following me home, so I shrunk to my twelve-inch size and snuck by the car, keeping to the little bit of shadow on the street. Once I was past the car and it was out of sight, I changed back to my normal size.

It was only a little over two miles from my business to my house, and I could walk through Glover-Archbold Park most of the way. Years before, it was usually full of trysting college students at night, but more liberal dorm-room policies changed that. High school kids had taken over that function in the park's ecosystem.

And since the Beltane catastrophe, there were predators. A girl couldn't even go for a walk by the river without being accosted by Vampires, Imps, Incubi, and the Goddess alone knew what might be next. Werewolves hunting squirrels and rabbits—and occasionally girls—were a constant irritant.

The park was part of the National Park system, so the DC Police didn't patrol the area. But the Park Police were more focused on ticketing people for littering than preventing assaults.

So, it didn't surprise me when an Imp leaped from a tree, hitting me in the back and grabbing the shoulder strap of my bag. If I had been Human, he might have gotten away with his theft. But I was already holding the strap, so the snatch-and-run didn't go off the way the Imp had expected. Although staggered, I managed to keep my feet. Holding onto the strap, I pulled the bag out of the Imp's grasp and backhanded him. The Imp flew across the trail and slammed into a tree trunk.

The impact didn't seem to faze him. Giggling hysterically, he bounced up and dodged around me, trying to grab the bag again. He came within reach of my legs, and I punted him thirty feet down the trail, where he landed and rolled head over heels until hitting another tree.

That gave me time to draw my sword.

"Nasty Elf," he said, springing to his feet. "You have so much and I have so little. Give me the bag and I will forgive you for hitting me." The Imp closed half the distance between us before he saw the gleaming sword and skidded to a stop.

"Bad Elf," the Imp gibbered. "Only a game. You would kill for a stupid bag?"

"No, I would kill you because you're rude," I replied.

"Ugly Elf," he spat. "Hope you never mate. Die all alone and worms eat your eyes."

Imps were loved only by other Imps, and for good reason. I sketched a rune in the air and spoke a Word.

"Noooooooo!" the Imp's cry cut off when he disappeared.

I let my sword slide back into its sheath and continued on my way. I had used the banishment spell so many times since the veils between the realms shredded that I didn't have to think about it anymore. It worked remarkably well on lesser demons, and occasionally on minor demons. Luckily, I hadn't faced any major or grand demons.

That the Imp wanted my bag wasn't a surprise. They were thieves and packrats, the crows of the paranormal world. And my bag would be quite a prize. The bag had been Alaric's, though I knew he stole it somewhere. Outwardly, it looked like a gaudily-dyed reptile skin bag with a shoulder strap, but inside was a pocket dimension that would hold more than I could possibly carry without it. A powerful mage crafted the bag from Dragon skin, and even in Alfheim it would be wildly expensive.

When I got home, I found another black Mercedes parked down the street where the two men inside could watch my front door. I wondered when I had become so interesting.

My lights were on a timer, similar to almost every house in the neighborhood. As though thieves wouldn't break into a lit house. My wards were far more effective, though I didn't want to stand out. I unlocked the door, and as I turned the knob, something white fluttered down to the step by my feet.

I picked it up and saw it was a business card.

After a glass of wine to accompany stir-fried vegetables with shrimp, I picked up the card from the table in the foyer and looked at it.

Abner Wilcox

Master Magician

Who in the hell was Abner Wilcox? And how did he and those creeps around the corner know where I lived? I decided that I did prefer sleeping where the Fairies were on guard, so before I went to bed, I put together some clothes and food to stock the cottage the next day.

That done, I went into my workshop to mix a few potions and store a few spells. I had discovered that paintball guns were a wonderful delivery mechanism for certain types of spells. I made up a large batch of paintballs especially for nosy busybodies.

The sky was starting to lighten in the east when I left the house the following morning. Landscaping crews started the day early, especially in Washington in the summer. It got too damned hot to work outside in the afternoon.

The black car was still parked where it had been the night before. A car was a terribly uncomfortable place to spend the night, and I wondered if the men inside were the same ones.

On an impulse, I walked up to the passenger side and rapped my knuckle against the window. The man inside startled, then looked at his partner. They exchanged a few words, and then the man near me rolled down his window part way.

"I don't think we've been properly introduced," I said. "I'm Kellana, but I assume you know that. And you are?" The inside of the car smelled like dog.

The driver started the car and slammed it into gear. I raised my paintball gun and fired a round into the back seat before the window rolled up. With squealing tires, the car sped away. I watched as the interior filled with pink fumes. Half a block away, the car started swerving, then jumped the curb, hit a stop sign, and continued into the wall of a house. It made an awful racket.

Lights came on in the surrounding houses, and a few people peeked out their windows or doors. Passing the Mercedes, I glanced inside it and saw both men lying unconscious, surrounded by a pink haze.

Humming an Elven marching song, I headed off to work.

Torturing the men parked by my house was so much fun, that I decided to try it again with the men parked by the nursery. But when I tapped on their window, the passenger's door swung open, hitting me and knocking me backward. The man inside pulled himself out of the car and reached for me. The driver also opened his door and sprang out.

Stumbling backward and trying to catch my balance, I fired a spell pellet at the ground between us. The Werewolf blundered into the fumes, swayed, and crashed to the ground.

His buddy didn't have much of a sense of humor. He drew a pistol and pointed it at me.

"Hold it right there," he growled. "Don't move."

That sounded like a bad idea. I dove to my left, hit the ground, and rolled. His gun fired, so I kept rolling, my cloak twisting around my body. The gun went off a second time. Afraid that the gunman might get it together enough to aim, I stopped. My arms were bound tightly to my body by the cloak, so I could neither reach into my bag nor sketch a rune.

"Okay," I shouted. "Don't shoot."

I fought to free my arms. The hood had twisted around my face and I couldn't see.

"Don't move," a voice near me said, and I froze.

I waited for something to happen, then I heard a sound like a shovel hitting a rock.

"Son of a bitch," a familiar voice said.

I fought free of the cloak and saw the driver lying face down. My friend Ed stepped over the Werewolf and picked up the pistol. He had a shovel in his other hand.

"Are you all right?" he asked me.

"Yeah, I think so."

Ed looked at the two men. "Who are these clowns?

"I don't know. They followed me yesterday, and then hung around all night. I think they have some friends—same make of car, same cheap suits—who were parked next to my house when I got home." I stood and looked around. It was very early, and I didn't see anyone on the street except my employees, staring wide-eyed at the men Ed and I had downed.

"Let's get them out of sight before someone calls the cops," I said.

Ed's head whipped around. "You're not going to call the cops?"

"Not until I have a chance to chat with these gentlemen and find out what in the hell this is all about. Then we'll call the cops. Get a couple of

16

wheelbarrows."

Ed grinned. He sent two of our employees after the wheelbarrows, and we loaded the Weres into them.

"Take them to the pump house," I said.

One of the girls who worked for me approached. "You're really a witch?" She glanced at the faint pink stain on the ground where the one Were had lain.

I chuckled. "After a manner of speaking. I'm an alchemist." I dug out one of the red spell balls.

"Looks like a paintball," she said.

"That's right. I buy them empty and fill them with my own concoctions. These red ones are a sleepy gas." A magically-infused sleepy gas. No need to go into the differences between witch magic and Elf magic.

"Why is it pink?" Ed asked as I walked over to the Weres' car. I took the keys and locked the car doors. Ed had worked for me for ten years, and he was quite aware that I wasn't a normal Human.

"It's special for he-men," I said.

Ed snorted and the girl giggled.

On the way to the pump house, I grabbed a handful of zip ties and bound the men's wrists and ankles, then strung three of the zip ties together. Dragging one of the men into a sitting position, I used the extra-long tie around his neck to bind him to a water pipe. Then I did the same with the other man.

Ed sent the crews out to their jobs and then came back. "What's with the neck ties?"

"They're Werewolves. If they shift, they might slip the ties on their hands and feet."

Ed's eyes got a little larger, and he nodded, but didn't say anything, just watched me as I finished securing the Weres.

17

The guy with the knot on his head recovered consciousness first. I knew the other one would be out for at least a couple of hours.

"Hi, handsome," I said, kneeling down in front of the one who was awake. "Care to tell me why you're following me around? Surely I'm not the prettiest girl in town."

The Were glared at me but didn't answer. I dug down in my bag and came out with my athame and a vial of silver dust.

"Ed? Where do you suppose the most painful place to apply a little fire would be?" I asked, holding the Were's eyes with my own.

"Oh, hell, probably his balls," Ed said.

"Nope," I answered. "Foreskin. I think I'll circumcise him, and then use this silver dust to cauterize the wound." I slipped the athame inside the man's belt and cut it. Next, I slid the knife inside his waistband and slit his pants open past his crotch.

"Will silver really kill a Werewolf?" Ed asked.

"Yeah. A silver bullet or an injection of silver into his vein would kill him. A little bit of silver sprinkled on a wound will probably cause his pee-pee to shrivel up and fall off, but it won't kill him."

I jerked down the man's underwear, and he bucked, writhing around and fighting against his bindings.

"You crazy fucking bitch!" he shouted.

I put the point of the athame under his chin and pushed just enough to break the skin. "Settle down, Fido."

He stopped thrashing, his eyes wide and staring at me. I knew the silver forged into the athame probably burned like crazy.

18

"Now. I believe I asked you a question," I said. "You shot at me. You tried to kill me. If you think that I feel any empathy or mercy whatsoever for you, then you're delusional."

"I didn't try to kill you. I just wanted to scare you."

"Uh huh. Just threaten me, huh?"

"Yeah, just to make you stop and hold still."

"I see. Well, let me tell you a little secret. I don't threaten. I make promises and I keep them." Ed knew about my ears, and other than the Were, he was the only person present. I pushed my hair behind my ear so the Were could see it. "Either you answer my questions, or I promise you I will cut off your foreskin and sprinkle silver dust on the wound."

I had often been amused by Earth myths about Elves. Yes, Elves were the epitome of tree-hugging environmentalists, but we weren't pacifists. Elves, Dragons, demons, Aesir, and Angels sat near the top of the predator-prey pyramid, one step below the Gods and Archdemons.

I watched the Were's eyes widen until I thought they were going to pop out of his head. He knew what an Elf was.

"I'm waiting," I said. "Why are you following me around?"

"The cat woman," he said.

"She told you to follow me?" I wiggled the athame a little.

"Find her. Find her," he babbled. "We need to find her."

"And why did you want me to hold still? Isn't that why you said you shot at me?" I dropped the point of the knife down to touch his penis.

"T-t-take you t-to m-m-y b-b-boss."

"And who is your boss?"

"Harold Vance."

I smiled. It must not have been very reassuring because he peed on himself.

"Thank you, puppy." I turned to Ed. "Now we can call the police."

We locked the Weres in the pump house and walked back to the office.

"Harold Vance?" Ed asked. "The guy with the big estate out in Silver Spring?"

"Yep. Top alpha wolf in the mid-Atlantic area. Organized crime around here is controlled by the Werewolves. And yes, we mow his lawn."

I didn't call the DC police, though. I called the PCU, the Paranormal Crimes Unit of the FBI. It took them about an hour, but five men in suits showed up in two cars and a van that resembled an armored car.

A man with dark brown skin, short curly black hair, and a broad nose approached me and held out his identification card.

"Miss Rogirsdottir? I'm Special Agent David Torbert of the PCU."

I led him to the pump house and opened the door. "These two men followed me yesterday, staked out my business, and this morning they accosted me." I handed him the pistol. "That one there fired two shots at me. Either you take them, or I'm going to use them to fertilize my monkshood."

Torbert chuckled. "Don't they also call that wolfsbane?"

I grinned at him. "I think that would make it extra potent, but I've never tried it. All in the spirit of scientific inquiry, of course."

"Well, in that case, I guess I'd better take them,"

he said. He turned and signaled for the rest of his men.

They came to the pumphouse, and I handed a pair of rose clippers to the first one as he stepped through the door. He looked at the clippers, then at the zip ties around the Weres' necks and grinned at me. After clipping the neck restraints, they carried the Weres out and loaded them into the big van.

"What happened to that one guy's pants?" Torbert asked.

"He was in some distress. I loosened his clothing," I said.

Torbert chuckled again. A lot of Humans didn't get my sense of humor, but I found myself liking Agent Torbert.

"I'm not going to ask whether his distress started before or after you loosened his clothing," he said.

I walked him back to his car. It took a while, as he seemed interested in everything in the nursery.

"I'm also not going to ask about what is going on here," Torbert said as he got in his car. He looked me up and down, taking in my six-foot-six stature, green hair, and slit-pupiled eyes. "I'm aware that Elves can't lie, but you're extremely adept at not talking about what you don't want to talk about." He handed me his card. "However, if you need any help, give me a call. I do appreciate that you respect our laws and didn't settle this yourself."

"Agent Torbert, I wish I knew what is going on."

CHAPTER 3

Cortez's card still sat on my desk. I hadn't looked at it before.

Dr. Isabella Cortez, PhD
Professor of Animal Behavior
University of Colorado

I dialed the number, and she picked up on the third ring.

"Isabella Cortez."

"This is Kellana Rogirsdottir," I said. "We need to talk."

"I will try to get there today." I thought I detected some distress in Cortez's voice. "Things have gotten more interesting since I spoke with you yesterday."

"That's an understatement. I'm being followed, and a Werewolf took a shot at me this morning."

"Oh, dear." She was silent for so long that I thought we had lost our connection.

"Dr. Cortez?"

"Yes, I'm still here. You have Werewolves, and I seem to have a wizard problem."

I took a deep breath, and then asked, "What kind of wizard problem?"

"I appear to be stuck here. I've tried to leave, but I'm not having any luck."

Before I could stop myself, my foolish mouth asked, "Do you need help? Would you like me to come and get you?"

"That would be lovely. Do you know where the Smithsonian Castle Garden is? I'm sort of trapped in here by some kind of spell."

"Are you under attack?"

"Not actively, no. But I can't leave. There are invisible barriers blocking off all the exits. No one else is here, so maybe people can't come in, either."

"It's eight o'clock in the morning. I don't think the museum is open yet," I said. "Hang on. I'll be there as soon as I can."

I decided to take my old Honda instead of one of the business's pickups. Maybe I could be a little less conspicuous.

I swung by my house on the way. My old workshop behind the cottage could still be used to mix spells, but I had moved all my ingredients to the new shop in my Georgetown house. My grimoires were also there.

A wrecker was in the process of towing the Mercedes away when I drove up to my house. The interior of the car was a lovely shade of pink that really didn't go with the black exterior.

Once I got into my workshop, I pulled out both my grimoire and Carolyn's. I had inherited the book along with the house when she died. The problem with her book was that my magic wouldn't execute some of the Human witch spells. But all of the potions, tonics, tinctures, poultices, and poisons did work.

Carolyn had been my one real friend in the Earth realm. We met about the time I bought the land for the nursery. Twenty years later, she invited me to share her house in Georgetown. She left me the house and a small trust fund to take care of the place when she died. Human lives were so short.

Quickly searching for something that could break wards, I came across a very nasty and loud spell that worked in conjunction with a potion. I had to mix two different solutions, then combine them at the ward while chanting the spell. The only problem was, I couldn't figure out from the description if the potion would simply dissolve the ward or take out a city block in an explosion.

Moving along, I found an elven rune-based spell. I wasn't sure if my magic was strong enough to take out the ward. When I said I wasn't a mage, I was telling the truth. I was a witch, with the magic any Elf had, plus a little more in some areas. I was a good alchemist, and I was strong in setting wards. I didn't have any experience at all in breaking them.

It might be a stretch to say Isabella had saved my life in that alley. I was fairly confident I could have escaped the Weres, but the fact remained that she had put herself on the line for me. I called Isabella back. To my relief, she answered.

"Where is the wizard who trapped you?" I asked. "Have you seen him?"

"Oh, yes. He's standing right outside the garden. He said that all I have to do is give him the artifact and he'll let me go."

"Do you have it?"

"No. I told him that, but he doesn't believe me. He thinks I know where it is."

"Would you be upset if I killed him?" I asked. I knew the wards would dissolve if the mage who cast them died.

"Not at all. I planned to do that at my earliest opportunity, but if you take care of the issue, I won't object. I've been here all night, and I'm starting to get hungry."

Stuffing my bow and quiver into my bag, I ran out to my car. I normally didn't carry the bow, since the DC authorities frowned on hunting in the city. But I didn't want to get in a magic battle with a real mage, and I expected an objection if I tried to get within sword range.

It took me some time to find a parking place near the Smithsonian Castle. Searching for a parking space was the city's most popular participation sport.

There were only three outside entrances to the garden, plus the one from inside the building. All three had wooden barricades erected across the sidewalk with "Garden Closed" signs on them. I circled around until I saw a man standing by one of them, then I called Isabella. I was a hundred yards away, and he didn't even notice me.

"Describe this mage who has you trapped," I said.

"Young, mid-thirties, dark hair. He's wearing blue jeans and a lighter blue shirt."

"Hazel eyes? Small scar over his left eyebrow?"

"I have no idea. I never got that close. He has a pistol."

I always forgot how poor Human eyesight was. Assuming Isabella was some kind of Human.

I walked up to the man and asked, "Are you holding someone against their will?" That close, I could feel his magic. He was a mage, and there was little chance I could break his ward, especially if he decided to stop me.

He whirled about, keeping one hand in the pocket of his light jacket. It was almost ninety degrees. No one needed a jacket.

"Who are you?" he asked.

"I understand that you're holding someone prisoner in there."

Pulling a pistol out of his pocket, he said, "You should mind your own business. Get the hell out of here."

That didn't sound very friendly, but I figured I had tried. That was the second time someone had pulled a gun on me that morning, and it irritated the hell out of me.

I did what he told me, walking away and crossing the mall to the other side. About two-thirds of the way to the street, I turned and looked back. There wasn't anyone close either to me or to the wizard. I knelt down next to my bag and slid the bow and an arrow out onto the ground. Taking a deep breath, I snatched them up, nocked the arrow, drew and loosed.

He jerked, arched his back, and fell forward.

"Isabella," I said into the phone, "run. Use the Independence Avenue exit and turn left."

I shoved the bow back into my bag, slung it over my shoulder, and walked away. I wondered if Agent Torbert would recognize an Elven arrow.

Circling around to Independence Avenue, I called Isabella again. We met on the street and hurried the three blocks to my car.

Isabella looked tired, and I remembered her saying she was hungry. "So," I asked as we drove away, "how did that happen?"

"He left a message at my hotel asking me to meet him. I got there, and didn't find anyone, but I couldn't leave. I tried all night, but no matter what I did, I couldn't get out. He showed up this morning at dawn and tried to get me to tell him where the statue is."

"Statue? You said you were looking for an artifact."

"It's a small statue."

A thought occurred to me. "Was that Abner Wilcox?"

She shook her head. "No, why? Where did you hear that name?"

"Who was it?"

"He said his name was Georges Tremblay. He said he was partners with Carleton Weber, the man who brought the artifact to DC."

More names, disconnected to anything. I had all kinds of questions running around my head. Who was Abner Wilcox, and why did he leave his card at my house? How did he and the Werewolves know where I lived? How did Isabella, or any of them, find me in the first place? Why were the Werewolves following me around? Who was the woman sitting next to me?

Danu merde, I had just killed a man. One question bubbled out of my mouth. "How did you know I'm an Elf?"

"I smelled you at the nightclub. I have met Elves before. There's a community of them in Colorado. Humans don't smell like flowers, no matter how much perfume they wear."

I stopped the car at a grocery store and we both went in. I bought fresh fruit, vegetables, and fish. She bought beef.

When we got to the nursery, I found my hibachi and started a fire in it. Cortez built the fire up and threw a huge steak on the grill. A minute later, she flipped it, and as soon as that side seared, she pulled it off onto a platter, sat down at my table, and demolished it. I cooked my small fish longer than she

27

cooked a steak two inches thick. Cats are obligate carnivores, so I decided I shouldn't have been surprised.

She accepted a cup of coffee and watched me as I ate my meal.

"I killed a man for you this morning. I think you owe me an explanation about this whole affair," I said.

Cortez regarded me in silence, then gave a deep sigh. "I asked you to trust me, and you did. I guess the least I can do is return the favor."

She proceeded to tell me a tale that most Humans on Earth would never believe, but it wasn't the most fantastic story I'd ever heard. I personally had seen more incredible things during my trip through one hundred eighty realms with Alaric.

Over a thousand years before, the god Acan attempted to seduce Ixchel, goddess of midwifery and war, called the Rainbow Goddess and the Jaguar Goddess. When she rejected him, he crafted a statue of a jaguar, cast with magic out of pure gold, and gave it to a great Mayan mage named Yash Kook Mo. The mage installed the statue in a secret room in the great temple at Tikal in Yucatan, and through an elaborate ritual involving human sacrifice summoned Ixchel. Acan knew that Ixchel couldn't refuse to bed one who summoned her, and that was his revenge. But there was a glitch. Magic always seeks a balance. When Ixchel appeared, so did the archdemon Camazotz, the death bat. Legend told that the Mayan practice of human sacrifice started as payment for Camazotz giving fire to the Maya.

In a battle that lasted for days, Yash Kook Mo defeated the demon and banished him. As a reward, Ixchel mated with him and bore him a son, then parted the veils and returned to her home. When the son grew up and became king, he carried out the ritual and called Ixchel as his father had commanded. Again, Camazotz was also called, and when the mage king defeated the demon, Ixchel mated with him and bore him a son.

"She mated with her son," I said.

"Yes," Isabella said, disgust showing on her face. "There's a certain ick factor to the whole story. Incest, Human sacrifice, murder—all the good stuff. I've studied tales of the gods, and they don't seem to have the same sense of morality as mortals."

For hundreds of years, this pattern continued, and the Mayans prospered under the rule of strong mage kings. Then Tikal was defeated in battle by the rival city-state of Palenque. The great mage king Janaab Pakal took the jaguar statue back to Palenque along with the secret of the ritual and the head of the Tikal king.

But when Janaab performed the ritual and called Ixchel and Camazotz, Ixchel was displeased that Janaab had killed her son and lover. She refused to help Janaab battle Camazotz, the demon was victorious, and Janaab was slain. Ixchel then mated with Camazotz but spited him by producing a daughter instead of a son.

Without the blessings of a great mage king, Mayan civilization declined. Camazotz demanded more and more sacrifices, and then called a drought upon Yucatan. The Aztecs and other barbarians soon reduced the Mayans to a subjugated people.

"Carleton Weber found the secret room beneath the Palenque temple and smuggled the statue out of Mexico," Isabella said. "I knew something had happened there, but I arrived too late. I followed him here to DC, where he had put the statue up for auction on the internet. When I finally tracked him down, he was dead, his home ransacked, and there was no sign of the statue."

"I thought you said you couldn't feel the statue. That's why you needed an Elf."

Isabella blushed and ducked her head. When she looked back up at me, she said, "I can't feel the statue. What I can feel is that room in Palenque. It hasn't changed in twelve hundred years. I didn't even know I could feel it until Weber opened the room and took the statue."

My mind sort of fogged as I tried to sort that out. Elves are exceptionally long-lived, commonly living a thousand years, so a being living that long wasn't what stunned me.

"You're the daughter," I blurted out.

"Yes, I'm Ixchel's daughter."

"The daughter of a Goddess and an Archdemon. A shape shifter. But you say you have no magic? You *are* magic."

"Well, yes, I guess you might say so. I have abilities beyond shifting, but they aren't magic, at least not in the way magic is usually defined. Do you consider your connection to plants and the earth magical?"

"No, of course not. But I use what some call Elven magic to shape plants and manipulate them."

"And I have certain powers, but they don't involve magic. I channel the Goddess's will and power."

"Ah, I see." And I did. Isabella asked the Goddess to lend her power, but the Goddess could say no. That was different than magic, which bent the natural world to the magician's will. But there was something Isabella didn't say.

30

"You said that Ixchel is the Goddess of midwifery and war. What are your powers?"

She licked her lips, then said, "You don't want to see them. I'll just say that for the most part, shifting to my jaguar form allows me to handle most problems."

I didn't want to push on something she didn't want to tell me, so I changed my line of questioning. If she didn't want to talk about her inheritance from her mother, I couldn't even imagine what she'd inherited from her father.

"You don't shift like a Werecat," I said.

Isabella shook her head. "No, I don't have to go through all that. Weres tell me that changing is painful. I know that watching them change is painful. It takes two or three minutes, stretching and pulling, their bones and muscles rearranging into a completely different animal. But I don't shift the way Weres do. It's almost instantaneous, a morphing that takes less than thirty seconds. I don't change mass, and my cat is far sleeker than my Human form."

"In the alley that night," I said, "I got the impression that your cat is larger than the Werecats I've known."

"The only cats larger than a jaguar are lions and tigers," Isabella said, without elaboration. Another dead-end line of questioning.

"So, you're afraid some mage will use the statue to lift the veils and bring this Camazotz into our world?"

She shook her head. "Not really. I suppose it's possible, but I'm the only one who knows the ritual to call Ixchel and Camazotz. And since I'm not a mage, performing the ritual would serve no purpose. Besides, eating human hearts isn't my thing. A mage might use the statue's power to summon other demons, I suppose, or create a portal to another realm. I don't know enough about that type of magic to understand what's involved."

Isabella gazed out over the park next to the nursery. We could see a band of Pixies hunting a beetle through the flowers on the other side of the fence.

"No," she finally said, "the problem is that the statue stores magic. Enough magic to breach the veils and reach all the way into the upper realms of the gods and archdemons, and its use involves blood magic. What I'm afraid of is giving that much power to someone who would spill blood. A novice mistake might blow a hole a mile deep and as wide as half of Maryland and Virginia. An experienced and canny mage could probably set himself up as a king. The fact is, it's an artifact of the gods, and doesn't belong in this reality."

CHAPTER 4

While I had my reservations about working with Isabella, it was obvious that simply being associated with her, however tenuously, had made me a target. That being the case, having her to watch my back made sense.

On the other hand, I wasn't crazy about having her in my house and making it a target, too. My Georgetown neighborhood was much too quiet and full of snoops and gossips to abide any more scenes such as the one with the Werewolves. But the cottage at the nursery had only one bedroom. I hadn't built it to entertain guests.

"Are you planning on going back to your hotel?" I asked.

"That doesn't sound like a very good idea, does it?" she replied. She surveyed the nursery, turning in her chair to look around. "This place is protected, isn't it?"

"Yes, I have wards set, and a Fairy nest is established here. I was curious as to why they didn't react to you. Normally they throw a fit when a paranormal attempts to enter the grounds."

"I guess I'm not a paranormal," Isabella said with a chuckle. "Would you mind if I stay here?"

"Well, I'm really not set up for company—" I started.

A smile spread on her face. "It's summer, and I'd be quite comfortable sleeping in one of your oak trees, if you don't mind. I'll be discreet."

An image of a jaguar lying on a tree branch came to mind. I wasn't sure if the image came from a

33

picture or maybe a TV show, or if it was something Isabella did.

"Yeah, sure. That will work." I pointed to the tree closest to us, behind the cottage. "This one is probably the best. That's a public park on the other side of the fence, and there are a lot of Pixies over there. Between the Pixies outside and the Fairies inside, I don't worry about anyone sneaking up on me."

"Thank you. Do you suppose I could talk you into a ride to the hotel so that I can get my things and check out?"

We drove down to the Willard, which was a stone's throw from the White House. Obviously, Dr. Cortez wasn't hurting for money, but it seemed a little strange to move from a five-star hotel into a tree.

I had never actually been inside the hotel before. The ornate lobby and plush carpeting covering the floors in the hallway leading to Isabella's room were far beyond anything I had ever seen except in a movie. When I traveled, it was always a low-budget affair.

Her room was equally impressive, but her luggage—a duffle bag and two backpacks—showed hard use. I helped her carry them down to the lobby and stood gawking at my surroundings as she checked out.

Outside, while we waited for the valet to retrieve my car, I felt magic. Once that had been a rare occurrence in the Earth realm. Glancing around, I saw a large man standing on the portico above us. He had gray hair, a long gray beard, and he wore a dark suit. It didn't take long to figure out that he was the source of the magic.

As soon as he noticed me looking at him, he moved toward us while raising his arms. I sketched a rune and spoke a Word. Isabella turned to face me, a frown on her face, then pivoted toward the object of my attention.

The mage's power lashed out, lighting the air around Isabella and me in a glow anyone could see. Very showy and very sloppy. Humans near us gasped and backed away.

"What the hell?" Isabella gasped, then her eyes narrowed as she focused on the mage. She started to step in his direction, but I reached out and grabbed her arm.

"Stay here," I said. "As long as you stay inside my ward, he can't hurt us."

The mage threw a second spell at us with a crash of thunder. People ran screaming in all directions.

"Are you sure?" Isabella shouted in my ear.

"Absolutely," I said in a normal, conversational-level voice. Her eyes widened.

"I thought you said you aren't a mage," she said, her voice much softer.

"I'm not. An Elven battle mage would wipe this guy from both reality and memory. But I don't need a warrior to protect myself." I didn't tell her that the mage's attack wasn't nearly as fierce as it appeared. He wasn't trying to harm us, only capture us. I considered if there was anything I could do to capture him.

Isabella stared at me for a few moments, then turned her attention back to the mage who was attacking us.

"You asked earlier about Abner Wilcox," Isabella said. "That is Abner Wilcox."

"Why is he being so nasty?" I asked. "And who in the hell is he? I mean, besides being Abner Wilcox. What's an Abner Wilcox?"

The mage stood less than ten feet in front of us, and I was sure he could hear our conversation. He turned so red in the face that I was afraid he might have a stroke.

"A mage and anthropologist," Isabella replied. "Doctor Abner Wilcox, PhD, University of Chicago. An academic rival to Carleton Weber, the man who looted the statue from Palenque."

"Why are there so many professors involved with this blood-magic artifact?" I asked. "Are all you people crazy?"

Isabella surprised me by laughing out loud. "Yes, I guess we are. Abner," she called to him, "you're making a fool of yourself, and if you don't stop scaring this young lady, she's likely to kill you the first chance she gets. Assuming I don't get to you first. Don't you think you should cut your losses before the police and the PCU get here?"

He snarled at us. "This isn't over."

Isabella snarled back, and he wet his pants. I almost wet my pants. The lady was spectacularly intimidating when she wanted to be.

Doctor Abner Wilcox turned and ran. Looking around, I saw my car idling next to the curb. The valets had fled along with everyone else.

Picking up Isabella's duffle bag, I dissolved the ward around us and said, "Shall we go before the police and the PCU get here?"

"Absolutely," she said, slinging the smaller backpack over her shoulder and picking up the larger one.

I opened the trunk, we threw her luggage inside, then jumped in the car. As we pulled away, we could hear sirens.

We unloaded Isabella's luggage and put it in the laundry room of my cottage, then I said, "I've been in this realm about seventy years, but I haven't had much interaction with your magic users. Is this Doctor Wilcox considered to be competent?"

Isabella laughed. "Actually, he is fairly well known, both as an academic and as a mage. I take it that you weren't impressed."

"That was a pretty loud spell he used to try and break my protection, and it didn't do anything at all. My friend Carolyn was much stronger than he is, and she didn't go around calling herself a master magician."

"Really? Maybe she could help us find the statue," Isabella said.

"Ah, no, that isn't possible. She died a few years ago."

I showed Isabella the bathroom and the laundry, which was a room off the business office. She seemed very interested in the grounds and expressed surprise at the pond, which covered almost an acre.

"I'm rather amazed that you have such a large lake here," Isabella said.

"It allows me to grow aquatic plants," I told her. "A lot of clients want koi ponds or waterfalls. I can raise my own plants instead of buying them, and I can experiment with varieties to find those that do best in this climate."

"Where does the water come from?" she asked.

I chuckled. "They drained a swamp to build Washington, D.C. It didn't take much effort to find an underground spring and redirect it to surface here. My water bills are nonexistent."

"I just can't get over what you've got here," Isabella said. "Right in the middle of the city." She gestured toward one of the oak trees. "Those trees at the four corners of your property. What was here before?"

"Vacant land. It's not exactly in the middle of the city, more like on the edge. Or it was when I bought the place from a developer. He planned to build houses here, but he ran into money difficulties. I planted the oaks."

She frowned. "I would have sworn those trees were hundreds of years old. They're huge."

"Elven magic," I said and grinned at her. "They provide very solid anchors for my wards."

Isabella craned her neck as she looked up at the oak nearest to us. "You said you came here seventy years ago, but you bought the place fifty-six years ago."

"I arrived in Germany. From there, I made my way to England and Ireland, then to New York. I spoke German with an Elvish accent, and English with a German accent. In the late forties, a great many people were uprooted without papers to prove who they were. I worked and saved my money. You know, for a large city, this one is more transient than anywhere else. The government changes on a regular basis. People move away, people move in. I've redesigned the landscaping at one house near Rock

Creek Park seven times for seven different residents."

"And being transient, people don't notice how permanent you are," Isabella said.

"I don't encourage close friendships. Probably the closest people to me are those who work for me."

"There are other Elves in the world."

I shrugged. "Now there are. Up until two years ago, there were very few of us. Those in Iceland and Colorado and New Zealand came from Alfheim. The Irish Elves came from Midgard. Most are noble refugees with their families and servants. I'm not of the nobility, and I have no desire to become a servant."

"Refugees?"

"Yes, there is war in Alfheim, and I suppose in Midgard as well. I've seen war, and I don't wish to see it again. I got excited when a lot of Elves came to this realm, but I've been here so long, I don't really have much in common with them anymore."

That evening, I watched Isabella change—the air rippled and a jaguar stood where a woman had been a moment before. She climbed my oak as easily as I would climb the three steps to my porch. She disappeared into the foliage, her rosettes breaking up her outline and providing camouflage.

I sighed and went inside the cottage, poured myself a glass of wine, took a long, hot bath, and went to bed.

CHAPTER 5

The next morning, I dropped Isabella off at a rental car agency, then went out to a prospective client's house in Fairfax County. It was a newly-built home with a lot of dirt, and judging from the size of the place, the client had a lot of money. I spent the morning brainstorming ideas with the lady of the house and told her I would email her some mockups in a couple of days.

I stopped by a café for lunch and planned on going by the new client in Chevy Chase for final approval of the plans and mockups I'd done for her. That's when my phone rang, and all of my plans for the day went to hell in the proverbial handbasket.

"Kellana!" Abbie Collins, one of the girls who worked for me, practically screamed in my ear. "Someone stole Sam!"

"Quieter," I said. "What do you mean, 'someone stole Sam'?" Samantha Watson, or simply Sam, also worked for me. The two women and three men formed a crew that had gone out to Bethesda that morning to do routine maintenance at two office complexes.

"They kidnapped her! Josh tried to stop them, and they beat him up." Abbie was clearly upset and half crying.

"Where are you?"

"Milton Corporation."

"Has anyone called the cops?" I asked.

"Yeah, Tommy is calling them. I think Josh needs to go to the hospital. Oh, my God, Kellana, he's bleeding! They beat the holy shit out of him. Why?

Why did they do that?"

"Abbie, try to stay calm. What did the men who kidnapped Sam look like?"

"Big guys. Business suits. They were driving the weirdest car. A black Mercedes with a pink interior."

I closed my eyes and tried to think. And then it hit me. Sam had been so proud when she showed up at work with green hair a few days before. The same shade of green as mine. She was also tall, though not nearly as tall as I was, and naturally blonde and fair skinned.

"We'll find her, Abbie. You guys take care of Josh and cooperate with the police, okay? I have to make some calls."

I hung up and called Isabella. As soon as she answered, I said, "Those damned Werewolves that were stalking me kidnapped one of my employees and beat up another one. I need to have a little talk with a guy named Harold Vance, and I need some backup."

"Who's Harold Vance?"

"He's a Werewolf syndicate bigwig."

"Crap. Where do you want me to meet you?"

"At the nursery."

I called Maurine and Ed to let them know what had happened. Maurine said she'd take care of Josh and the hospital. I sent Ed to Milton to take care of the rest of the crew. Then I stopped by the Georgetown house to change clothes and add a few wolfsbane paintballs to my arsenal.

Isabella was waiting for me when I pulled into the nursery. We left the car and took one of the service trucks. If I had to run into anything, I wanted solid steel bumpers, not the plastic things on my Honda.

"Why do you think they kidnapped her?" Isabella

41

asked as I negotiated traffic on our way to the Beltway.

"She dyed her hair green."

"Oh. Obviously not the correct fashion decision."

"No, but she couldn't have known it would make her a target, and I didn't even think about it. I was just happy when punk rockers started using colors in the eighties, and I could stop dying my hair."

"So, where are we going?"

I was still thinking about that. Vance owned a number of businesses and was reputed to run them all from a strip joint in Largo, outside of the District near the football stadium. His home was closer, an estate-sized place in north Silver Spring.

"How much do you know about Werewolves?" I asked Isabella. "Would a Were be at his strip club business in the middle of the day, or at his home, frisking around the swimming pool with his harem?"

"Interesting question. Which one is closer?"

"His home."

She shrugged. "Let's go there first. If he isn't there, then we haven't lost any time. Do you know where it is?"

I grinned. "I have a contract to do the grounds maintenance. I probably won't after today, but I know the setup like the back of my hand."

While we drove, I filled Isabella in. Vance's place covered about two and a half acres, surrounded by a ten-foot brick wall. About an acre was covered in forest, the rest was mostly lawn. The area around DC was overrun with deer, and Vance had a gate in the back wall that he usually left open to encourage the deer to come inside the wall, where he and his pack usually ate them.

"Is ten feet too high for you?" I asked.

She laughed. "Not at all. You?"

"Not a problem."

I parked down the road from Vance's front gate, which was open. I could see a couple of men through the window of a small gatehouse just inside the wall. I didn't intend to go through the gate, though.

Isabella watched me load my two paintball guns and strap on my sword.

"What's in the paintballs?" she asked.

"A sleepy-gas spell in the red ones. The silver ones are a wolfsbane potion. Lethal to humans as well as wolves if they ingest it. The potion is geared toward Werewolves, though."

For the first time, I wondered if Isabella could be harmed. Common wisdom was that Gods and Archdemons were immortal. "Can you be killed?"

"I don't know. I assume so," she answered with a lopsided grin, "but no one has managed it yet. I definitely bleed and hurt, and I wouldn't want to try your little potion. But if we can talk the locals into shifting instead of using guns, then I'll be just fine."

The way she said, 'just fine', made me shiver a little, and I remembered the Weres in the alley the night we met.

We walked up to the wall, about fifty yards from the road. I hopped up on top of the wall and looked around. A jaguar landed next to me but stayed only a few seconds before leaping to the ground below.

A number of people and wolves lounged around the pool in the back of the house fifty yards away. Several children and puppies splashed in the water. I didn't see Vance, but I did see his wife lying on a lawn chair in a bikini. For a brief moment, I wondered if

Werewolves got skin cancer.

I took my bow out of my bag, slung the quiver over my shoulder and pulled an arrow from it. I wanted to get their attention, but not hurt anyone. I finally found a target, drew and loosed. The arrow made a satisfyingly loud 'thunk' as its head buried itself in the beer cooler.

All sound ceased. Everyone looked around, trying to figure out where the arrow came from. Then one of the kids shouted and pointed at me.

My second arrow broke a glass sitting on a table next to Vance's wife. Things got very quiet again.

"I'm looking for Harold Vance," I yelled. "He kidnapped one of my employees, and I want her back. Tell him I'm out here."

Several of the wolves started in my direction, and I saw several of the people begin to shift. One man pulled a pistol from a shoulder holster. My third arrow hit him below the collarbone just inside the point of his shoulder. The pistol clattered onto the ground.

Everyone was staring at me, but about that time the first wolf realized that a large cat was standing in his way. He barked. Isabella roared. All the children started crying, and all the puppies either hid under something or ran in the opposite direction. The adult wolves froze.

"Where is Harold Vance?" I shouted.

"He's not here," his wife shouted back.

My fourth arrow impaled the cushion of the chair between her legs. "That wasn't what I asked."

She stared at the arrow quivering in front of her. Her mouth worked, but only a croak and an incoherent whimper emerged.

"He's at the club," a man called.

"Tell him to stay right there," I said. "And tell him if he hurts the girl, I'm coming back here when I finish with him." Isabella leaped to the top of the wall, turned, and let out another roar.

We jumped down from the wall and sprinted toward the pickup. I felt a faint sense of regret that I hadn't recovered my arrows. It took almost a day to make each one.

When we reached the truck, Isabella changed to her human form, then opened the door and jumped in. I started the engine and whipped a U-turn.

"They'll be waiting for us," Isabella said.

"And if Vance has any sense, Samantha will be waiting for us outside his club," I said, then sighed. "Probably not. A lot of the Weres and Vampires were born here. Their ancestors crossed through the veils centuries ago, and their children have no sense of history."

Her brow furrowed and she gave me a searching look. "I'm not sure I get your point."

"Until a couple of thousand years ago, Elves used the realms near Earth—among them Transvyl and Were—as sport-hunting grounds. We've become a bit more civilized since then, but people who grew up in those realms would be far less likely to piss off an Elf."

Humans inhabited almost all the realms. I had grown up with them in Midgard, so I knew their limitations and their strengths. But the Weres and Vampires I had met tended to look at Humans as prey, which was a dangerous assumption. Humans and Elves looked alike and could interbreed, so often non-Humans thought of us as a type of Human, and therefore a type of prey. That kind of thinking often proved fatal.

45

I parked four blocks from Vance's club, The Wolves' Den, and we took to the shadows. I was surprised at Isabella's dexterity and flexibility. She was at least a foot shorter than I was, but she outweighed me. She also kept up with me when I scaled a building, leaped from roof to roof, crossed a highway, and slipped through a grove of trees. From the shelter of the trees, we peered across the road to the club sitting at one end of a small strip mall. Next to the strip club was a liquor store, then a sex shop with a peep show, and then a gas station with a convenience store.

"I don't see a green-haired girl standing out front," Isabella said.

"Yeah. So much for wishful thinking."

"So, what's plan B?"

"I walk in and get her," I said. "You wait outside, and if it sounds like things are going badly, shift and come in after us."

"You're joking."

"No, I'm not." I turned toward her. "Look, Isabella, they want me because of my association with you. It makes absolutely no sense for you to go in there."

"Yes, but they were willing to kidnap you, and now you're just going to walk in?"

I smiled. "I can't cast a glamour on you, but it's something any Elf can do to themselves."

The light went on, and a smile grew on her face.

Donning a glamour that gave me Ed's appearance, I crossed the road. As I pulled the door open, I looked back and saw Isabella trot across the road, angling to the side of the club. When I stepped inside, I released the glamour and shrunk down to my smaller size.

Hugging the shadows, I inched my way around the room.

A dancer with a bored look on her face strutted around on the stage accompanied by loud rock music. Fewer than twenty customers sat around a room that could hold two hundred. A bouncer sat at a table about twenty feet inside the room. He turned toward the door when it opened, but not seeing anyone, he turned back to watch the dancer. Beyond him, a bartender wiped the bar with a towel. He didn't seem to be in a hurry, watching the dancer and not what he was doing.

I wasn't much of a judge for such things, but I decided the girl on the stage was probably pretty. She had long legs and large breasts.

The whole club smelled like the Mercedes—like dog.

The building was two stories, but there wasn't any staircase that I could see. Edging my way along the wall, I set my sights on a door at the back of the room with an 'Employees Only' sign on it.

As I made my way forward, I noticed that all of the customers were keeping one eye on the front door. The bouncer and the bartender were also a lot more alert than they appeared at first. I wished that I'd set up a better signal for Isabella to crash the party. Too late. Technology such as cell phones didn't work well when magic was twisting reality, and my shrinking and glamour were definitely not part of Earth's normal reality.

It took me about ten minutes to reach the back door, then I turned to face the room. No one appeared to be looking at me. I grew back to my full size, drew the paintball gun with the sleepy gas, and fired five paintballs into the room. Twisting the doorknob, I backed through the doorway and closed the door.

I found myself in a short hallway with a door on either side. A small, empty office showed through one open door. The other doorway opened into what looked like a break room and a changing room for the dancers. At the end of the hall was a stairway leading up.

When I reached the bottom of the stairs and looked up, I saw a closed door with two thugs standing outside. One of them opened his mouth, and I fired another red ball at the door. Both thugs sank to the floor as the pink mist engulfed them.

I waited until the mist settled, then climbed the stairs to the door. The knob moved when I twisted it, so I pushed the door open. Vance sat behind a large desk, and six of his men stood around the room. One more sat next to Sam on a couch. She looked a little disheveled and sported what would probably turn into a black eye. I saw red.

"Ah, Miss Rogirsdottir," Harold Vance said. "I'm so glad you could join us. It seems my men mistook—"

It took me only two steps to reach him, so he didn't get to finish the little speech he had evidently rehearsed. My left hand clutched his throat, pulled him from his chair, and slammed him against the wall. My right hand drew my sword.

The Werewolves were slower. Only about half of them had their guns drawn when Vance hit the wall.

"If you ever touch one of my employees again," I said through gritted teeth, "I will be carrying your wife's head when I come to talk with you." His eyes widened in fear. "Tell your men to drop their guns. Now. I can *hear* the click of a trigger, and I'll be gone by the time a bullet gets here, but you won't be."

His voice sounded a little strangled as he said,

"Drop your guns. Do it now!"

I counted six objects hit the floor. I knew there was a man to my left, and I hadn't heard a thump from that direction. With a long step-pivot off my left foot, I swung around, and my sword took off the Were's arm between his wrist and his elbow. The clatter of a pistol hitting the floor sounded as I swung back.

"Sam, are you okay?" I asked.

"Y-yeah. I guess so."

"Which guys beat up you and Josh?"

She pointed to the two men who had staked out my house in Georgetown.

"Stand up and go downstairs and out the front door," I told her. "My friend Isabella is waiting there for you. Tell her that if I'm not back in ten minutes, to come and get me."

"Okay," she said, standing and walking to the door. "Thanks, Kellana." Her voice broke a little, then I heard her steps on the stairs.

"Now," I said to Vance, "you and I are going to go somewhere private and talk. Your thugs are going to stay here. Understand?"

He nodded. I grabbed him by the hair and pushed him in front of me toward the door. As I passed the two Weres Sam had pointed out, I swung my sword and disemboweled one, then took the head of the other on the back swing. I heard a gasp from more than one of the remaining Weres.

Vance stopped and stared at the men I had killed. The headless one toppled, and the other dropped to his knees, his hands clutching his belly, trying to keep his intestines from spilling out on the floor. I prodded Vance in the butt with the point of my sword, and he hopped toward the door.

"Where's an empty room?"

"Down here," he said, indicating a room at the end of the hall.

I put the sword point between his shoulder blades. "Lead on."

The room was empty. From the rumpled covers on the bed, I assumed it was the place where he bedded his dancers. I pushed him toward a chair and told him to sit.

"So," I said, leaning against a wall with my sword point resting on the floor, "you wanted to talk with me. Now's your chance. Talk."

He stammered around until the last thin thread of my patience snapped.

"You're looking for a statue," I said. "Why? You can't use it."

Vance squirmed and looked uncomfortable.

"Do you even know what it is?" I asked. From his face, I could tell that he hadn't a clue. "You idiot. Who's the mage who paid you to steal it?"

I laid the blade of my sword across the back of his hand. His skin sizzled like bacon, and he tried to jump back, but the chair was backed against a wall.

"Mr. Vance, I'm not a cruel person. I would prefer to go about my business, and not have anything to do with you or blood mages. But you have attacked me and people under my protection. Unless you cooperate with me, I shall be forced to conclude that you are the source of my problems. And if I can solve my problems by removing you from this reality, I shall do so."

"My pack would avenge me," he snarled.

"You are assuming there will be a pack tomorrow morning."

The shock in his eyes told me I was finally getting through to him.

"You aren't powerful enough to take on three hundred Werewolves."

I smiled. "You will never know." I could see the outline of a cell phone through the material of his suit. Reaching inside his jacket, I pulled it out and put it in my bag.

Seven minutes of silence followed. Right on cue, I heard the roar of a jaguar from downstairs. Vance jumped in his seat, his eyes wide in panic.

"My friends have arrived," I said. "I'm sorry, Mr. Vance. I really despise the slaughter of women and children, no matter what race they're from. But you leave me with no bargaining chips. What am I to tell the demons when they ask who is hiding the statue?" I sighed. "I'm just a small part of all this, and I don't have any control over what those far more powerful than me might do."

I turned toward the door.

"Karl von Wagner," Vance blurted out. "He offered to pay a million dollars for the statue."

"And who offered to pay more?" I asked. I didn't believe for a second that Vance would go to all this trouble for a million. "Come now. Surely you have the bids submitted to Carleton Weber. You got those when you killed him and took his computer."

Vance shook his head. "I didn't kill Weber." He took a deep breath. "Akari Nakamura offered two and a half million. I figured that we could get the bidding higher."

"Weber thought that, too. Don't assume you can

protect yourself better than he did. Just look at what one Elf can do, and then think of what might happen if one of the great wizards or a demon decided to twist you. I would advise you to lose interest in that statue."

I walked out, calling, "Isabella, I'll be right down."

CHAPTER 6

Sam awaited us in the woods across the street. I put my arm around her and hugged her to me.

"You're all right?" I asked, and gently touched the swelling around her eye.

"Yeah, I'm okay. How's Josh?"

"I don't know. We're going to go find out."

"Who were those guys?"

"Criminals. I'm so sorry you got mixed up in this. They seem to think I know something, but they're wrong. It's the same group of thugs who tried to kidnap me at the nursery the other morning."

"I picked a good time to dye my hair, didn't I?"

I chuckled. "Your timing isn't that great, but I am flattered."

"Yours isn't dyed, is it?"

I drew away from her a little and scanned her face. Although she was understandably shaken up a little, I saw strength there. She was a survivor.

"No, this is my hair. Can you keep a secret?"

She nodded. I pulled my hair back so she could see my pointed ear.

"I'm not exactly Human," I said.

"I kinda figured that out. More human than those goons back there, though," Sam replied.

I smiled. "Thank you. I do need you to be discreet about what you saw today."

"Not a problem. Kellana," she said, the expression on her face very earnest, "some people think that all the beings who came across the dimensions are monsters, but most of us don't think that. We know

53

that a lot of you are good. Everyone who works for you knows about the Fairies, and Fred and Kate. We see you with the plants." She shrugged. "We all know you're from somewhere else."

I called Maurine when we got back to the car. She told me that Josh was sedated. The doctor promised to call her when they judged him ready for visitors.

We drove to the nursery, where Ed and the rest of Sam's crew were gathered. Special Agent Torbert was there as well.

"Miss Rogirsdottir," Torbert said. "I see that you found your missing employee."

"Yes, she turned up," I answered.

"I'll need to speak with her. We do take kidnapping seriously, and we'll need her cooperation to find the people responsible for this."

"That won't be necessary," I said. "The matter has been resolved."

He pursed his lips and then frowned. "I thought this might be connected with the incident the other morning."

"Are those men who assaulted me still in jail?" I asked.

"No, they bailed out."

"One of the more stupid practices your society engages in. Letting criminals buy their freedom so they can commit more crimes."

"I hoped you might allow the law to handle this matter," he said.

"Agent Torbert, many of the beings who came here from other realms don't respect your laws. If I can't protect my employees, they won't respect me, either. I gave you a chance to show me your laws work, but you let a pair of kidnappers go free. As I said, the situation has been resolved."

Isabella and I swung by the hospital that evening to see Josh. The doctor told me that Josh had two cracked ribs, a mild concussion, and a lot of bruises. They planned to keep him overnight and discharge him the next morning. Sam showed up as we were leaving and declared him a hero. I don't think he noticed when I left.

"You impressed Samantha," Isabella told me as we waited for our meal at the steakhouse where we went for dinner.

I laughed. "In what way? She barely said hello."

Isabella shook her head. "Not at the hospital. At the strip club. When she came out, she said that you were 'kicking ass and taking names'."

My face suddenly felt hot. "She really said that?"

The shifter nodded. "You surprised me at Vance's estate. I didn't have you pegged as a warrior."

"Elves don't have the kind of gender divisions Humans have here on Earth," I mumbled. "We all learn to use weapons and how to hunt when we're growing up."

"And how to intimidate people? How to assault an enemy castle?"

My training had been a bit beyond normal, but my father was a retired queen's guard. I didn't want to talk about the five years I spent walking the realms with Alaric, or what I had to do to survive in Germany. Alaric was a master at running a bluff, and I had a ringside seat for a lot of his schemes. Also, for the occasions when his schemes went wrong, and we had to fight our way out.

"Werewolves are easy due to their pack dominance hierarchy," I said. "If Vance had been in his wolf form, I probably would have had a fight on my hands. But all I had to do was overpower one person, and all the rest tucked their tails between their legs. The only alpha at Vance's home was his wife, and she's all looks and dominance. Dumb as a brick."

I shrugged. "A lot of races would simply ascribe it to natural Elven arrogance. We naturally assume we are the smartest, strongest, most beautiful people in the room and that everyone will bow down to us. But we're very modest compared to Angels."

Isabella snorted, then she changed the subject. "So, what did you learn at Vance's club?"

"More names of people looking for the statue. That doesn't do us any good. I'm beginning to think everyone in town is looking for it. You said that Weber died and his home was ransacked. Were you there?"

"Afterward. I estimate that he'd been dead at least one, maybe two, days when I found him. The hard drive had been taken from his computer, and the house looked like a tornado hit it. Whoever searched it was very thorough. The mattresses were cut open, every drawer and closet was emptied, and the refrigerator was dumped out on the floor."

"Smells?" I asked.

Isabella gave me a raised-eyebrow half-smile. "The rotting food was lovely. But if I were to run into the man who killed Weber, I would recognize his scent."

"When was this? Do you think the police are still hanging around?"

She shrugged. "A couple of weeks ago. Why?"

56

"You said you can't feel magic. If the statue was under the floor or buried in the back yard, you would have missed it."

"That would assume the person who killed Weber couldn't feel its magic either, otherwise, why tear the place apart?"

"I'd still like to see his house, his car, his office, and anywhere else he might have had the statue. Maybe I can pick up some residual. Otherwise, we're blundering around in the dark along with everyone else."

Isabella looked thoughtful. "Maybe you're right."

"Look, people are trying to question you and me simply because they think we might know where the statue is. We know that we don't know where it is, so why wander around chasing other people who don't know where it is?"

She burst out laughing. "Okay, let's try something different."

We drove to Weber's house near George Washington University and parked one street over. The house still had yellow crime scene tape around it. We snuck into the backyard and I forced the door. As soon as we stepped inside, I realized that no one had cleaned the place. The stench of the rotting food from the refrigerator had become almost overpowering.

I sketched a rune and spoke a Word. The smell of lilacs blooming filled the house.

"Thank you," Isabella said. "Wow, that is a magic I would love to have."

We searched through the house, and I saw that Isabella hadn't exaggerated. The previous search or searches had been exceptionally thorough. Two old trunks in the attic had their contents strewn about without any care at all.

The basement, where Weber had his workroom, was a different story. I could feel the remains of spells and wards, along with certain magical artifacts and ingredients. A few things I pocketed. Phoenix feathers were impossible to find on Earth, as was the dragon scale. I wondered where Weber had acquired such items. Some things I found led me to believe Carleton Weber was not a nice man. The only way someone could collect a bottle full of Pixie dust was to stuff a Pixie in the bottle and wait for it to starve to death.

We stepped carefully through the kitchen and through a door into the garage. Weber's SUV practically glowed with residual magic. A powerful object had been transported in that car. The magic, tainted with blood and stinking of demon, threatened to turn my stomach. If that was the statue I smelled, I would recognize it if I got close to it. My face must have shown my feelings.

"Do you feel something?" Isabella asked.

"The car. It transported something that left traces of blood magic and demon."

"So, you wouldn't have a problem identifying the artifact?"

"No, but I certainly wouldn't want to touch it."

With that as a guide, I made a quick circuit of Weber's yard.

"I don't think the statue was ever here," I told Isabella. "It was in the car, but it never made it into the house."

I wanted to visit Weber's office, but Isabella suggested that a daytime visit would be more prudent. "During the day, there are people everywhere at a university, and no one will notice us. But the office buildings will be deserted at night, and the campus police will be curious."

When we got back to the nursery, I found several Fairies waiting for me at the cottage. It took me a while to derive the gist of what they were upset about, but I finally figured out that a man with magic had approached the fence from the park and tried the wards. I rewarded them with a piece of chocolate and they headed off to get drunk.

Isabella disappeared up the oak tree, and I went to bed.

CHAPTER 7

Samantha showed up for work on time and told us that the doctors were probably going to let Josh go home in the afternoon. She also said his parents were flying in that morning. I told Maurine to find out when their flight was due and drive them to the hospital.

After the crews headed out on their assignments, I left Ed in charge at the nursery. Isabella and I drove to George Washington University.

Professors' office locations were easily found on the internet. The Archeology Department was located in a row of red-brick buildings that housed administrative offices, offices for professors and graduate students, laboratories, and classrooms. As Isabella predicted, a lot of people were coming and going, and no one gave us a second glance. I knew that I was less noticeable on a college campus than anywhere else on Earth.

Weber's office was on the third floor of a building, a bit isolated and quiet compared to the lower floors. I heard someone typing in an office a couple of doors down from his office, but otherwise I couldn't detect anyone's presence.

"It's rather early," Isabella said in a quiet voice. "Can you get through the lock?"

I grinned. Laying my hand on the electronic keypad, I let magic flow into it. As often happened when I tried to program any kind of electrical device, the keypad went crazy and stopped working. With an audible click, the door unlocked.

We stepped inside and closed the door. In contrast to the chaos at Weber's house, it didn't look as though the office had been searched. Passing through a second door, we found Weber's lab. The amount of magic from magical items and residual magic from other items was almost overwhelming. But the stench of blood magic mixed with demon scent managed to seep through everything else.

"I don't think it's here," I said, "but it was. There are a lot of magical artifacts here, however."

I began going through drawers and cabinets and closets. I found jewelry, pottery, statuettes, weavings, plus gems and crystals that either stored magic or were magical in themselves. Almost all of them had a feeling of age.

"Weber's been collecting magically-enhanced objects for a long time," I said.

"It was the focus of his work," Isabella said. "He was known in archeological circles for his emphasis on religion and rituals in ancient cultures. In paranormal and magical circles, he was known for his obsession with magical artifacts."

Picking up a pendant with a large moonstone, I asked, "Do I have to leave all this here?"

Isabella shrugged. "I don't care. As far as I know, the university is still debating how, and whether, to incorporate paranormal studies into their curricula. Found something you like?"

I held up the pendant. "It has a protection-against-magic charm." Pointing to a small, rough-carved statuette that looked like a pregnant gargoyle, I said, "That thing needs to be thrown in the ocean. It's filthy, and I would hate for anyone to use it."

"Any idea what it does?"

"Yes. It uses blood magic to kill things—animals and plants. It was created out of jealousy and spite.

It's the kind of thing that dark mages with small minds create."

"Wonderful," she said. "How do we transport it?"

I held up a silk bag that I'd found. "Put it in here. Try not to touch it directly. We'll drive out to the Bay and chuck it overboard."

She looked dubious. "It won't hurt the fish or water plants?"

"No, it would need to be activated, and salt water will prevent that. It's the kind of simple blood spell that any idiot could perform. But it will sink to the bottom and hopefully be buried in the mud forever."

Isabella took the bag and slipped it over the little carving. "How old is it?"

"Ancient. Thousands of years."

When we walked out of the building, Isabella asked, "So, what now?"

"We know where it isn't," I said. "Either Weber stashed it somewhere, or his killer has it. What else do we know about Weber? Did he own a vacation home or a boat? If he was trying to sell the statue here in Washington, I wouldn't think he'd hide it too far away. But first, we get rid of that hideous fetish."

"And where do you plan to do that?"

I grinned. "Have you had a chance to sample our wonderful Chesapeake Bay blue crabs?"

We took Highway 50 toward Annapolis and then to the Bay Bridge.

"How good is your arm?" I asked. When I received a blank look, I clarified. "How well can you throw?"

An equally blank look with a bit of a head shake was my answer. "I don't know. Why?" Isabella said.

I pulled over at a gas station, filled up the truck,

and when we got ready to leave, I said, "You drive."

As we pulled out into traffic, I said, "I think we're being followed." The same car had been parked outside the Archeology buildings.

"The blue car?" Isabella asked. "I thought it was kind of a strange coincidence."

"Just drive, and once we get on the bridge, stay in the right lane."

At the apex of the bridge, one hundred eighty feet above the Chesapeake Bay, I rolled down my window and threw the ugly fetish carving as hard as I could over the railing. I twisted in my seat and watched it drop into the waters below.

The blue car, two cars behind us, slammed on its brakes, skidded, and was rear-ended by the car behind it. A chain reaction crash followed.

"Wow," Isabella said, looking in the rearview mirror.

"Don't watch them! Watch the road!" It had taken a true act of faith to ride over that bridge with someone else driving. I tried not to be a control freak, but high bridges scared the hell out of me. Too many drivers like the fool in the blue car.

"Yes, mother," she replied with a sly grin.

We drove down to St. Michael's and ordered a dozen crabs for lunch. Isabella figured out how to crack them a lot quicker than I did my first time. On the other hand, she ate everything but the shells. I ate only the meat. On our way back, the radio alerted us that one side of the bridge was closed due to a wreck, and the other span was carrying two-way traffic.

I managed to make it to the hospital as Josh was

checking out. I met his parents and assured them that I would take care of all the bills, including their hotel and rental car, while they were in DC. It was the second summer that Josh had worked full-time for me, and I wanted him and all of my employees to know that I stood by them. Hopefully, the Werewolves had learned their lesson.

That night, I was awakened by the Fairies. When I went outside to see what the problem was, they told me that the same man had come back and tried magic to get past the fence again. He hadn't been any more successful than the previous night.

The following morning, I spoke to Isabella about our visitor. She was sitting in my kitchen working on her laptop when I came back from setting up my crews for the day.

"If he comes back tonight, I'm thinking of preparing a surprise for him," I said.

She grinned. "I've been staying inside your fence, but that tree has limbs that hang over the park. So, what kind of surprise do you have in mind?"

"I can't throw fireballs or direct lightning, or anything showy like that," I began, "but I can manipulate plants. And most mages, human mages at least, don't seem to have much interest in that sort of thing."

Isabella looked out the window at the oak tree. "How fast can you make things grow?"

"There are varieties of bamboo that grow a foot a day during their growing season. With a little encouragement, I can push that to several feet a minute. If I set the rhizomes today, they'll be ready tonight. The idea is to fence him in and then see what happens."

"Should be fun." She motioned to her computer.

"I was reading the news about that crash on the bridge yesterday. The driver of the blue car was Abner Wilcox."

"I wondered if he was the mage coming around here at night."

"Not last night. He's in the hospital. He's not hurt too badly, but he's in Annapolis. Reading between the lines, he should be out either today or tomorrow. He'll have to get another car, though." She held up her laptop so I could see the picture of six cars piled up. Wilcox sat on the ground near his car talking to a cop.

"Wonderful. So, my stalker here is another stupid mage who thinks we have the statue."

"Sort of looks that way."

A number of plants grow from rhizomes, which is a modified plant stem. Among them are irises and bamboo. I grabbed several bamboo rhizomes from storage, hopped the fence, and planted them along a twenty-foot stretch of the fence near my cottage and about ten feet from it.

A number of Pixies came to investigate what I was doing, and I gave them a few sugar crystals while explaining that my nighttime visitor was not a friend. Pixies were far wilder and more savage than Fairies, and truth be told, not nearly as intelligent. Like Fairies, they were extremely territorial.

I spent most of the morning preparing the mockups for the client in Fairfax County and emailed them to her, then drove over to Chevy Chase to meet with the client who I'd stood up when Josh and Sam were attacked.

The woman in Chevy Chase attempted to talk me down from my price, but when I started showing her how we could scale the project down, she quickly backed off. Bargaining over cost was one human behavior I had never understood. An Elf set a fair price, and either you wanted it at that price, or you didn't. Not that Elves were always honest. Alaric never worked for anything that he could steal instead.

I drove back to the nursery, frequently checking my rearview mirror. Being followed was becoming all too common. I was surprised, however, when I parked at the nursery and discovered that my follower was Agent Torbert.

"To what do I owe this pleasure?" I asked as he got out of his car.

"I got a tip that a couple of Werewolves met an untimely demise. I tried to talk to Harold Vance about it, and he said he didn't know what I was talking about. But my informant was adamant that an Elf had declared war on the shifters."

"Why, Agent Torbert, I didn't know you believed in Elves. Do you believe in Santa Claus, also? Isn't he the guy who employs all the Elves?"

He glared at me. "According to all of the witnesses, the men who beat up one of your employees and kidnapped another one were Werewolves."

I shrugged. "I wasn't there. The doctor didn't say anything about a dog bite, but I'm sure that if you apprehend them, Josh and Sam will try to make an identification."

"That's the point. My informant says the Weres are dead."

"Oh. Well, I'm sure they don't look much different than when they were alive."

Torbert took a deep breath, his chest swelling impressively. "Miss Rogirsdottir, I have information that a murder has been committed. I'm asking you if you know anything about it."

"Oh, well, why didn't you say so. You just said some Weres had died. Who was murdered?"

His complexion was very dark, but it got darker, and it seemed as if his eyes bulged. I got the impression he was angry with me. Or maybe just frustrated. I hoped it was the latter. I tried to stay beneath the notice of Human authorities.

"Would you like some lemonade?" I asked. "I do. Why don't you come in while I make it?"

I turned and walked away from him toward my cottage. After I'd taken a few steps, I heard him start to follow me. Isabella's rental car was gone, so I didn't have that complication to explain to the special agent.

He stood in the doorway and watched me make the lemonade, dump some ice into a couple of glasses, and pour it. I handed him a glass.

"It must be frustrating to have your understanding of the universe turned upside down, and all these strange creatures invade your world," I said.

"You might say that," he replied. "I know that many non-Humans have lived here for a very long time."

"Until the veils shredded at Beltane."

"Yes. It's been a little crazier since then."

"Agent Torbert, my advice is to worry only about what non-Humans do when it involves Humans. Otherwise, let them settle their disputes between themselves."

"Your employees are Human."

"Yes, they are. The dispute didn't involve them. They were just in the wrong place at the wrong time."

"So, you admit that Werewolves were involved."

"I admit that Samantha was mistaken for me. I admit that Harold Vance is a client of mine. My company maintains the grounds at his home in Silver Spring, and I declare that income on my taxes. I admit that I am aware of non-Humans inhabiting this realm. I am willing to admit a great number of things, Agent Torbert. Would you like some more lemonade?"

He glanced at his glass almost in surprise that it was empty.

"Uh, no. Thank you. I guess if you don't have anything to tell me, I should go."

I took his glass and walked him to his car. "I'll tell you something far more important than why a couple of idiot Werewolves died."

He stopped and turned to face me.

"There are a number of mages gathered in this town, looking for an ancient artifact," I said. "At least one of them is willing to kill for it. Any of them who truly understand it, and are still looking for it, are probably willing to kill for it. If you hear of such an artifact, I would suggest contacting me. You really don't want to handle it or allow anyone to keep it."

"What kind of artifact are we talking about?"

"A golden cat. Someone might be tempted for the gold. That would be as foolish as trying to sell a ball of plutonium. Trying to use magic with it would be as foolish as putting that plutonium in a bomb. You could have another Beltane of two years ago on your hands. Possibly worse."

He shot me a look of surprise, then cocked his head. "You're serious."

I nodded. "Don't let someone get bureaucratic and try to keep it, or give it to someone to study, or stick it in a museum. Bring it to me, and I'll see that it's disposed of properly. It doesn't belong in this realm."

"Why are you telling me this?" he asked.

"You wanted me to tell you something important. Good day, Agent Torbert."

CHAPTER 8

I turned off the lights around ten, then climbed up the oak with Isabella. It was rather unnerving being with her in her jaguar form. I didn't expect that I would ever forget what she did to those Weres in that alley the night I met her.

Shortly after midnight, Isabella made a low, grumbling sound. I looked and saw a dark shape coming across the park toward us. As it came closer, I was able to see that it was a man. His scent revealed that he smoked tobacco.

He stopped about five feet from the fence, almost directly under the limb Isabella and I lay on. I drew a rune and began stimulating the bamboo. The first shoots poked through the soil, then they began to shake a little, as though disturbed by a breeze. They began to grow behind him, and soon were taller than the man they encircled.

He loosed a blast of what felt like electricity. The ward absorbed it. He followed that with a fireball, which blazed along the surface of the ward for thirty feet in all directions until it dissipated. His power impressed me. Without the oaks anchoring my wards, he might have broken through. The thought struck me that it was a good thing I'd decided to stay at the nursery instead of my house.

He pulled a bag from his pocket and began drawing a pentagram on the grass with chalk. Then he stepped inside the star and began to chant. I didn't recognize the spell he was spinning, but it didn't sound like something to break a ward. Of course, he'd tried to break in two nights in a row and failed.

A glow surrounded his body, and he started to

70

levitate into the air until he rose above the fence. Then he moved forward until he hit my ward. The glow seemed to interact with the ward, causing a ripple, like wind on water. I could feel the power he poured into the ward as if I was being buffeted by a high wind.

Isabella roared and leaped from the tree. She hit him from behind, and there was a flash, like an explosion, but without any sound. They fell to the ground and lay still. I stared at them with my mouth hanging open, completely stunned at what she'd done.

Shaking myself out of my paralysis, I dropped to the ground, taking care not to drop into the pentagram or to touch it. The jaguar lay half inside the pentagram and half out of it. I muttered a prayer to the Goddess that Isabella still lived. I found I was holding my breath until I saw her chest rise and fall. Hopefully she wasn't permanently damaged in any way.

A Fairy hovered above my shoulder, and when I looked up I saw it was the queen.

"Rhoslyn, do you know if it's safe to pull the cat out of the circle?" I asked.

"I have no idea." The diminutive woman flew down and hovered over Isabella, then dropped her spear. It stuck in the jaguar's shoulder and stood there. Nothing happened. Rhoslyn flew around the spear several times, then reached out and snatched it, flying up and away from the big cat. Nothing happened.

The Fairy queen flew back to me and said, "I think it's safe, at least if you use a rope or something to pull her with. I don't know if I would touch her with my hand."

"Could some of your folk bring me a rope?" I asked.

She flew up and over the fence. Ten minutes later, a couple of dozen Fairies flew down to me carrying a twenty-foot length of nylon parachute cord.

With the Fairies' help, I slid the cord under Isabella's shoulders and tied it. Then I dragged her out of contact with the pentagram. As soon as she was free, I saw Rhoslyn throw her spear at the mage. The ward flared as the spear passed through it, but the spear did pass through and stuck in the mage's neck. Rhoslyn turned to me and shrugged.

I was as puzzled as she was. If the ward was still in place, the spear should have bounced. I picked up a pebble and tossed it. Once again, the ward flared, but the pebble did bounce.

Rhoslyn cheered and called her people. Before I could do anything, a dozen Fairies had launched their spears through the ward. More Fairies poured over the fence, and in less than a minute, the mage looked like a pin cushion with six-inch spears sticking out all over him. Blood covered his face and hands. He didn't move, though I could hear him breathe. I sketched a rune at the four cardinal points as I walked around the outside of his pentagram, then spoke a Word and set a ward.

I bent down to check Isabella, and although her breathing and heartbeat sounded normal, I couldn't rouse her. Picking her up wasn't a problem, but once I had her in my arms, I knew I was never going to jump over the twelve-foot fence carrying a two-hundred-pound jaguar.

"If he wakes up while I'm gone, don't let him leave," I called to Rhoslyn. She gave me two thumbs up. Her people sat around the pentagram, on top of the fence and in the branches of the oak, many with nectar wine or chocolate, watching the mage and waiting for him to wake up. The air was charged with the festive atmosphere of a grand entertainment.

I carried Isabella around the property to the gate, about five hundred yards. By the time I got there, she seemed to have tripled in weight. I stared at the keypad to open the gate and tried to figure out how I could punch the keys with Isabella in my arms.

To my surprise, a Fairy swooped down and danced on the keys. The gate clicked and swung open.

"Thank you," I said. She giggled and took off in the direction of where the mage was imprisoned.

I put Isabella in a garden cart and wheeled her to the cottage, then carried her inside and laid her on my bed. Her breathing and heartbeat were still regular, but she hadn't roused at all. My healing skills ended with mixing potions and poultices and dealing with a magical shock was beyond my knowledge. Hopefully, she would come back.

I got my bow and sword, then went back outside and climbed up the oak to the place where I'd watched the mage before. In addition to the Fairies ringing him, the local Pixies had taken up seats on the bamboo leaves.

He was coming around, moving and moaning. I hadn't clearly seen his face as yet. In addition to the blood and Fairy spears, he wore a black hooded cloak, which was a bit warm for my taste during a Washington summer. I could see his hands, so I knew it was a man.

About fifteen minutes after I resumed my perch, he abruptly sat up and looked around. He was a white man, appearing to be in his late fifties or early sixties. I didn't recognize him. His hand brushed his face and found all the Fairy spears embedded in him. He looked at his hands and the spears sticking out of them. The Fairies all broke out laughing.

His eyes widened as he took in his Fae audience. He bolted to his feet and left the protection of his pentagram only to run into the ward I had placed around him.

"Good evening," I called. "How nice of you to drop in. If you had called ahead, we would have prepared a welcome feast for you."

The Fairies thought that was funny.

"Oh, well, I guess we did prepare a welcome, didn't we? I'm Kellana, but I'm afraid I didn't catch your name."

He raised his hands and attempted to use some kind of spell against the ward, but I didn't see any effect. It looked to me that he was either exhausted and drained, or my ward had cut him off from the source of his magic. Whatever the reason for his spell's failure, the panic on his face was easy to see.

A Fairy threw a spear that hit his eyebrow. A dozen Pixies threw their spears, too.

"You bitch!" he screamed. A Pixie spear pierced his tongue.

"Oh, my. You really should watch your language. You're actually lucky you still have your eyesight, but if you continue to act like an ass, I can't guarantee your safety."

He tried to say something, but he couldn't pull his tongue back into his mouth because of the four-inch spear.

"Perhaps I should just go get some sleep, have breakfast, then come back and see if you're in a better mood," I said. "I'm sure it will hurt pulling those spears out, but they aren't barbed."

I stood on the branch and started walking back toward the trunk inside my fence.

"Wait!" he yelled. At least, I think that's what he said. I turned and saw him with his tongue hanging out of his mouth and his fingers attempting to pull on the tiny Pixie spear embedded in his tongue. He pulled it out and swore. Blood dribbled out of his mouth to join the blood already running down his chin.

"Yes?" I asked.

"You're not going to leave me here!"

"Actually, I am. You're rude, uncooperative, and you attempted to break into my property. Because of that, I assume you're a thief. I should probably call the PCU, but I'm not always a nice person. I think a day without food or water will probably make you more communicative."

I turned away and continued walking along the limb. He howled and cursed, but I ignored him, confident that he wasn't going anywhere. I was halfway down the trunk when I heard a blood-curdling scream, then Fairies and Pixies giggling, then silence. I assumed the little people got as tired of his voice as I was.

Isabella was still unconscious. Whether she was sleeping, wandering another realm of consciousness, or brain dead, I couldn't say. I sacked out on the couch.

I woke to noises coming from my kitchen. Opening my eyes, I saw that the light was on. After listening for a minute, I decided someone was making coffee, an activity that received my highest approval.

Swinging my legs down to the floor, I stood and made my way, the five steps necessary, to see what was going on.

Isabella punched the on button of the coffee maker and turned toward me.

"Hi," she said. "How did things go after I checked out last night?"

"I'll let you see for yourself after breakfast. What in all the realms did you think you were doing? Goddess forbid, jumping into an active pentagram? Didn't your mama teach you better than that?"

She laughed. "She wasn't around much. I take it that wasn't the smartest move I've ever made."

"I'm surprised you're alive. A Human or Elf doing that would probably be dead, or brain dead at the very least. Goddess, Isabella, don't do things like that. Couldn't you feel the power he was generating?" Of course, I reflected, that would assume an Elf or Human was able to breach his protection enough to touch him. She should have bounced.

"Um, actually, no. He just stood there mumbling, and then he started to glow a little and rose up into the air. It looked like he was trying to levitate over the fence, so I thought it was a good time to ambush him."

I gaped at her. "*Danu merde.*" I described the magical displays I had witnessed, including the glowing power the mage funneled into my wards at the moment she attacked him.

"Nope, didn't see any of that. So, did he get away?"

With a chuckle, I started digging food out of the refrigerator. "Not hardly. I'm starving, but we can go see our prisoner after we eat. He wouldn't give me his name, but maybe you know him."

"You know, I could see what Abner Wilcox was doing, and so could other people. Why not the guy last night?" she asked.

"This guy would wipe the floor with Abner Wilcox. Wilcox put on a show on purpose, trying to intimidate us. That's what you do when your power is as limited as his is."

She cocked her head. "Can you always see and feel power? It seems like you know what a person is or can do just by looking at them."

I felt my face get a little warm. "Well, yeah, but I'm sure that other magic users do the same thing. I feel their magic with my magic."

Isabella shrugged, but the narrow-eyed look she gave me made me feel guilty, though I hadn't done anything to feel guilty about.

"None of the other magicians or paranormals I've known could do that," she said.

After breakfast, we climbed the tree again and made our way to the spot over the mage. He sat on his cloak on the grass inside my containment spell with dozens of tiny spears lying around him. He was covered in dried blood, and everywhere I could see his flesh, it was marked with red cuts. With his cloak off, I could see that my original guess at his age was close. Salt and pepper hair, clean shaven, and enough lines in his face to convey experience but not age. He was rather handsome, if a girl went for blood mages.

"Good morning," I said, taking a bite of an apple. "I slept well, how about you?"

He gave me a dirty look. Surly. But he didn't say anything. I turned to Isabella and cocked my head in question.

"Nope, I don't recognize him," she said, "but that

77

doesn't mean anything. I don't keep track of all the two-bit thieves who think they have some kind of magical skill."

The look he shot her was poisonous.

"So, what should we do with him?" I asked. "Just leave him here until he rots? That would be very stinky. Or I can call the PCU. I don't know what they would do with him. Probably say he's on public land and hasn't committed any crime."

A buzz erupted from the Fae, and especially the Pixies. In their eyes, he was a trespasser who had used magic illegitimately. They thought he should be punished.

The mage looked around at all the little people calling for more of his blood, and I thought I saw a little fear seep into his defiant posture.

"You don't know who you're dealing with—" he started, but my laugh interrupted him.

"No, I don't," I said. "I've asked repeatedly, and you refuse to tell me. So, let me explain a few things to you." I pulled out my bow and an arrow. "When I get tired of you, I'll turn you into mulch. I don't plan to lower my wards, and I don't plan to feed you. The forecast today is in the nineties, with DC's lovely humidity, so I expect lack of water will probably get to you before hunger. And I don't feel even a small bit of sympathy for a blood mage. The ball's in your court, asshole."

"You're a hard woman," Isabella muttered.

"When I have to be," I replied under my breath. "He scares the hell out of me. This guy is no lightweight."

"I'm not a blood mage," the mage said, indignation dripping from his words. "Whatever gave you that idea?" I thought I caught a bit of a British accent.

"Why are you trying to break into my nursery? Why not walk through the gate during business hours? Are you so poor you can't afford a daffodil, so you have to steal it?"

He growled at me. Isabella growled back, and he looked a little shocked.

"What are you looking for, señor?" Isabella said. She changed into a jaguar, then changed back. "You want a little jaguar? I'll give you a little piece of tail." He blanched, and she turned to me. "Just like a man. All tough talk and no performance."

I had to stifle a laugh, but the Fairies and Pixies rolled around, laughing and spinning in the air.

"Look," I said, "we know what you're looking for, and we don't have it. As to why I think you're a blood mage, only a blood mage, or a complete fool, would want to have anything to do with the thing."

"That wasn't nice," Isabella said. "You just called the funny little man a complete fool." She peered down at him. "I think it's a lot more likely that he's just a liar."

"I assure you, Dr. Cortez, that I am neither." Maybe not British. Not Irish. Australian?

A Fairy near me yawned. I had to agree, the mage was becoming tiresome. I nudged Isabella in the ribs with my elbow.

"I'm bored. Let's do something more fun. We can come back tomorrow and see if he's easier to deal with."

We left him there and climbed down the tree. I went to my office and took care of paperwork. Isabella took her laptop to my kitchen. Around noon, I noticed that the usual number of Fairies were out among the flowers. They didn't have very long attention spans, so that made sense.

After dinner, Isabella suggested a trip to the bar where we had first seen each other. The same Irish dance band was playing, and I was tempted. First, though, I scaled the tree again.

I felt a twinge of pity as I looked down on him. He sat slumped in the middle of the blackened pentagram. As I predicted, it had been a hot day, and for long stretches, there wouldn't have been any shade from the oak or the bamboo.

"Feeling any more talkative?" I asked.

He jerked and craned his neck to look up at me. His lips moved, and smacked together, and I realized that without any water, his mouth was probably too dry to work properly.

"You can kill me," his voice came out in a croak, "but there will be others. We won't rest until that abomination is destroyed."

"Are you speaking of Isabella?" I asked. "You'll never get a date by calling her an abomination."

"Make your stupid jokes. In the end, you'll discover your folly."

"Oh, hell," I said, and pulled out my phone. I called Agent Torbert. When he answered, I said, "This is Kellana Rogirsdottir. Do you have any mages on staff?"

"We have a couple," Torbert replied, "and a couple of witches. Why?"

"I have a mage that tried to break into my place and assaulted a friend of mine. I don't know what to do with him."

Said mage could hear only my side of the

conversation, but he was listening intently.

"If I press formal charges, will the PCU lock him up, or are you just going to let him pay money to get out, and I'll have to deal with him again?"

"PCU?" the mage squeaked.

"I can't guarantee we'll hold him," Torbert said in my ear. "Unless there's a compelling case for keeping him locked up, he's probably entitled to bail."

"Damn. Agent Torbert, I really don't want to kill him, but I also can't spend my life looking over my shoulder."

"PCU? Don't call the PCU!"

"Hold on a minute," I told Torbert and put my hand over the phone. "What the hell do I do with you?" I asked the mage. "I figure I have two choices, kill you or turn you over to the authorities. Make your choice."

The mage leaped to his feet and held up an identification card. A human wouldn't have been able to read it at that distance, but I didn't have a problem. I turned back to my phone.

"Agent Torbert, what is the Pontificium Consilium de Artium Arcanum Mortis?" I wasn't sure I was pronouncing it correctly. I did recognize it as Latin, a language I'd never studied.

"It's...well, sort of a trade association."

"Like a guild?"

"Yeah, I guess. In English, it's the International Council of Arcane Arts, headquartered in Romania. They say they regulate magic users, but that's more wishful thinking than reality."

"So, they think they're the good guys?"

Torbert chuckled. "Don't we all? Is that who the mage you captured is? One of their agents?"

"Sort of looks that way. His name is Vincent Crocker. Look, do you think you can come out to my place and talk to this guy? I'm not sure what to do with him, and he doesn't seem to want to leave me alone."

I heard what sounded like a full-blown guffaw on the other end of the line, then a chuckling Torbert said, "I can be there in about twenty minutes."

CHAPTER 9

"You called who?" Isabella seemed a little upset with me.

"The PCU, the Paranormal Crimes Unit of the Federal Bureau of Investigation. They're sort of your national police, I think."

She gave me a disgusted look. "I know who they are. Why in the hell did you call them?"

"What am I supposed to do with that guy? He's some kind of agent—" I didn't get any farther.

"The gods-bedamned ICAA. The self-appointed arbiters of all that's holy and right. Hell, I'd as soon deal with blood mages."

I was confused. "But he said—"

"Yeah, I'm sure he said he only wanted what was best for humanity. Think about it, Kellana. Are you Human? Am I Human? We're the people the ICAA wants to protect humanity against. They're a bunch of damned bigots."

"Okay, so we can let Agent Torbert deal with him."

"Oh, yeah, the bloody PCU. Two peas in a pod. The difference between them is they each think they're more holy than the other, but they have the same goal—get rid of all the non-Humans."

I heard a car drive into the compound and looked out the window. Agent Torbert and another man got out of the car, along with a very short woman. They all wore business suits. The other man and the woman were much lighter skinned than Torbert. The man had brown hair and was thinner and a bit taller than Torbert. The woman was even shorter than Isabella, thin, with long straight black hair to her waist.

Isabella followed me when I walked out to meet them, but hung back, watching.

"Miss Rogirsdottir," Torbert said, "this is Special Agent Alan Bronski and Special Agent Karen Wen-li. Miss Rogirsdottir is the owner of this business and the one who called us."

I went through the ritual of shaking everyone's hand. I had never understood it, but Humans tended to get offended if you didn't want to touch them. Bronski was a shock, a mage of some power, but uneven and cold in flavor. Wen-li was a witch whose power was warm and comfortable, like my mother's. I reminded myself that although her power felt that way, my mother was not always warm and comfortable. She could be hell on wheels, as Humans said.

I saw the three Humans glance at Isabella, but since she didn't seem to want to be introduced, I didn't try.

"Where is this ICAA mage you're worried about?" Torbert asked.

Since I wasn't going to lead that party up my tree, I led them out the gate and around through the park.

"He's technically not on my property," I explained as we walked, "but three nights in a row he tried to breach my wards and break in. Last night, he assaulted a friend of mine when she tried to stop him."

"How are you holding him?" Bronski asked.

"I cast a containment circle around his pentagram."

Bronski and Wen-li gave each other a long look. Evidently what I said meant something to them, but I didn't know what.

The bamboo was twelve to fifteen feet tall. I held out my hands as I walked into it. A path cleared through it and closed behind us, which caused more looks between the two magic users and garnered raised eyebrows from Torbert.

"When was this bamboo planted?" Wen-li asked.

Without thinking, I said, "Yesterday morning. After he showed up two nights in a row, I figured he'd be back. I wanted to complicate his retreat."

Arriving at the clearing where Vincent Crocker sat, I discovered that only a few hard-core mage watchers remained of the Pixies and Fairies. Three of the Fairies flew to my shoulders and started telling me, all at the same time, about what the prisoner had been doing while I was gone. The three PCU agents gaped.

"Well, here he is. He's fairly strong—not your average hedge witch. You'll need something other than one of your standard cells to contain him."

Torbert looked uneasy. "I'm not sure we can hold him."

"I'll file charges. Breaking and entering, and assault. Not to mention that he's rude."

At that, all the Fairies and Pixies started talking at once, telling the Humans that Crocker was rude. From their point of view, that was his major offence.

The Humans stared at the little people as though they had never seen them before. I thought about it and decided that actually might be the case. Everyone who visited the nursery seemed entranced by my Fae friends.

"Water," Crocker croaked.

We all turned toward him.

"How long has he been here, without food or

85

water?" Wen-li asked.

"Since about one o'clock this morning. He wouldn't talk, wouldn't tell me his name or his business. It wasn't until I threatened to call the PCU that he identified himself. He begged me not to call you." I couldn't help a smile spreading on my face as I had the chance to ask, "Do you torture prisoners? He was very upset about me calling you."

Torbert barked out a laugh, then said, "I hate to disappoint you, but no, we don't torture prisoners. What are all those scabs on his face and hands? Where did the blood come from?"

"Spears?" Wen-li pointed to all the tiny spears on the ground around Crocker.

"Well, yeah. The wee folk are rather territorial," I said.

"I never saw a containment spell surround a pentagram," Bronski suddenly said. "What kind of spell did you use?"

I fidgeted. I didn't like to talk about magic with Humans. "I just set a ward around him," I finally said. "Runes invoked at the cardinal points, like the ward I have around the nursery."

Bronski looked up at the oak tree, then through the fence at the oak at the opposite corner of the compound, then at the bamboo towering over us. Then he looked at Wen-li and said, "This is a completely different kind of magic than any I've ever seen."

She smiled at him. "I've seen it before. I'll tell you about it." Turning to Crocker, she said, "If we let you out, will you behave yourself? No international incidents?"

"Yes," he said, his voice almost a gasp.

86

"I think you can let him free," Wen-li told me.

I spoke a Word, then looked up at the Fairies sitting on the lowest branch of the oak. "I'll pay in chocolate if you bring me one of the green water bottles. One that's full of water."

A couple of dozen Fairies took flight, rocketing over the fence toward the supply shed.

"Chocolate?" Wen-li asked with a grin.

"It's like whiskey to them. Just a little bit gets them very drunk. Their queen thinks I'm a bad influence, but as long as I don't go overboard, she looks the other way."

A couple of minutes later, the Fairies brought the bottle, carrying it in a hammock contrived of a scrap of weed-barrier fabric.

"Thank you!" I said as I took the bottle. I counted the six Fairies carrying the bottle and the six supervising. "As soon as I'm through with these people, I'll get the chocolate from the cottage."

They cheered, and whirled away, I assumed to sit on the kitchen windowsill and wait on me. I tossed the water bottle to Crocker.

"That is amazing," Wen-li said as she watched the Fairies fly away.

While that was going on, other Fairies and Pixies had been darting down, grabbing spears from the pile around Crocker, and then flying away. About half of the spears had been retrieved.

I drew Torbert aside. "Remember the story I told you about the golden jaguar?" He nodded. "I think Crocker is after the statue and thinks I'm hiding it. He said something about destroying it. I'm not sure a nuclear explosion could destroy the damned thing."

He stared at me, his eyes searching my face as

though he could read something there. "I find that difficult to believe. What kind of object is that thing?"

With a deep breath, I said, "Are you religious, Agent Torbert? Do you believe in one god like a lot of humans do?"

"I guess so, though I don't consider myself very religious. My girlfriend is a pagan."

"That artifact belongs in the realm of the gods. It was used in blood magic rituals to summon gods and demons. I'm told that it contains immense power. I've never seen it myself, but I have been in a place where it was stored. I would rather sleep with carrion and rats than be near it."

"If that's the case, what do you plan to do with it?"

"Give it to a demigod who says she can return it to where it belongs."

His eyes shifted toward Isabella for an instant.

I grinned. "Do you really think she looks like a demigod?"

The PCU agents bundled Crocker into their car and drove away. Isabella gave me a scowl and said she was going to one of the university libraries. She didn't say when she'd be back, so I assumed our night out to listen to music was cancelled. I grabbed a historical romance novel from my to-be-read stack, then poured myself a glass of wine and a bath infused with lavender oil.

"Get up. I have a lead."

I opened my eyes and tried to focus on Isabella, but it was very dark. I checked my internal clock and found that I'd been asleep only for two hours. Combined with two long days in a row, I wasn't feeling very lively.

"Can't it wait until morning?"

"No, it can't. Come on. Get dressed."

"Easy for you to say," I grumbled as I sat up. "What kind of lead?"

She handed me her laptop. At first, I couldn't make sense of the pictures on the screen. It looked like a war zone. Syria or Iraq, maybe.

"What is this?"

"Arlington."

"*Danu merde.* Now?"

"Yes, now. It just happened about an hour ago. I need you to tell me if the magical signature matches what you felt at Weber's house and lab."

I tumbled out of bed and grabbed clothes from my closet. Arlington was just across the Potomac River from the Capitol and all the main government buildings, a suburb packed with apartment buildings and residential areas.

"Where in Arlington?" I asked as I pulled on a shirt and bent down to pick up my boots.

"As best I can figure, somewhere between the Pentagon and Reagan National," Isabella said.

I stopped. "We don't have a snowball's chance of getting there. Not unless you suddenly develop teleportation or learn how to fly. The military will be all over that area."

She stared at me, frustration plain on her face.

"What makes you think magic caused this?" I asked.

"They're saying that the blast zone is almost a mile wide, and damage extends another mile past that."

89

"No mushroom cloud?"

She shook her head. I had to agree with her. I couldn't imagine any kind of Earth-origin bomb that could produce that kind of devastation.

"These pictures are from the fringes of the destruction," Isabella said. "The photographer was at the airport."

I took a deep breath and tried to think. There seemed to be only one answer.

"If you want my help, then we have to go through the authorities. There's no way we can sneak in there without permission. Hell, they may detain us and think we did it. The U.S. military isn't big on magic users, from what I've heard."

She bit her lip, and I gave her time to think. "You think your PCU friends could get us in there?" she finally asked.

"It's worth a try. The worst they can do is say no."

I could hear her teeth grinding together, but with a jerking nod, she said, "Okay. Call them."

Although it was one o'clock in the morning, Torbert answered his phone immediately.

"Yes, Miss Rogirsdottir?" He sounded hurried and impatient.

"My friend thinks the explosion in Arlington was caused by the golden jaguar."

"Okay. Look, I'm really..." his voice tailed off. "Can you repeat that?"

"We think Arlington was caused by someone trying to use the golden jaguar I told you about."

"Why did you call it an explosion?" he asked.

"Isn't that what happened? I'm looking at photos on the internet."

"Magic." His voice held a musing note. "How would we tell if this was caused by your artifact?"

"I would have to get close to the scene. I know what the jaguar feels like. If the damage was caused by magic, it will have left residual traces."

"Where are you?"

"At the nursery."

"I'll have a car pick you up." He hung up.

I looked at Isabella. Her hearing seemed to be as sharp as mine, so she should have heard Torbert's side of the conversation.

She nodded. "Finish getting dressed."

CHAPTER 10

A black SUV with FBI plates pulled up outside the nursery gates. Isabella and I slipped through, and I closed the gate behind us. A burly man wearing a helmet and a flak jacket sat behind the wheel, and Karen Wen-li was in the other front seat.

We jumped in the back, and the driver pulled away, turning on red and blue emergency lights and a siren.

Karen twisted around to face us. "Dave said you told him about a magical artifact. Can you give me any more information?"

I glanced toward Isabella. After giving me the evil eye, she sighed and said, "It's an ancient statue that was used in certain ceremonies more than a thousand years ago. Blood ceremonies. Sacrifices. It stores magic. An archeologist took it from a tomb about two months ago and brought it to DC. He tried to sell it and ended up dead. The statue disappeared, and unfortunately, a lot of mages are interested in acquiring it."

"And you think it caused the incident in Arlington?" Wen-li asked.

"Can you think of a non-magical event that would cause such a catastrophe?" Isabella countered.

Wen-li's eyes shifted toward me, then back to Isabella. "And who are you?"

"Doctor Isabella Cortez, University of Colorado. I'm a zoologist with a specialty in animal behavior. I also have an interest in ancient Mesoamerican civilizations."

"Ah, the shifter expert," Wen-li said. "I've read a

couple of your books." She glanced back at me, then continued. "Dave said that you warned him about someone trying to use the artifact. Your warning and what happened are much too close for coincidence."

"Isabella is the one with the knowledge," I said. "She's the one who thinks it's so powerful. What I can tell you is that I have been in a place where we think the statue was, and it stinks of blood and demons. I've never felt anything like it, and I've been in Hel."

Wen-li nodded, then asked, "Hell with one 'l' or two?"

"One."

She made a face and turned back around.

Our driver took us on the most direct route, down the GW Parkway, across the Arlington Memorial Bridge, and then south to the Pentagon. At that time of the morning, there wouldn't normally have been much traffic, but we did see a lot of police and military vehicles. When he pulled off the road and parked, Wen-li got out and we followed her, looking around in disbelief.

Trees were blown over, and some looked as though they had blown in from somewhere else. Full-grown trees. The trees still standing were bare of leaves. Debris covered the ground. I saw a spec of color and walked over to it to find half of a child's doll. The buildings I could see were standing, but they had taken a beating. The flashing lights of police, fire, and ambulance vehicles gave the whole scene a surreal look.

Torbert met us and asked, "How close do you need to be to tell us anything?"

"I don't know. Is this near the center of what happened? I can't feel anything here."

93

"No," he said. "We're on the periphery. For half a mile from what we're calling ground zero, everything is flattened."

"Worse than this?" Isabella asked.

"Much worse."

"*Madre nos protégé,*" she breathed. "How many people?"

Torbert stiffened, and for a second, as I watched his face, I thought he was going to crack. "Tens of thousands. At least," he said and turned away.

I started walking forward, but before I went very far, a soldier stepped in my way.

"You can't go any farther, miss," he said.

I turned and looked back at Torbert. He stepped up and showed his identification. "She's a special consultant, Sergeant."

The soldier shook his head. "I have my orders, sir."

It took half an hour and half a dozen phone calls, but finally some soldier with stars on his shoulders and a superior of Torbert's got together and talked for a while. When they finished, a dozen soldiers spread out in front of me and started walking forward. Torbert, Wen-li and Bronski approached Isabella and me.

"Follow the soldiers," Torbert said. "They'll supply security."

I traded a look with Isabella and rolled my eyes but didn't say anything. I was faster than any of them, and I had no idea what they might be protecting me from.

As we walked, Torbert told me, "ICAA threw a fit about us arresting Crocker, and we received a complaint from the English ambassador. Rather than deal with them, my superiors decided to deport him."

"So, where is he now?" I asked.

"That's the thing. Some of our men took him to the airport, but he must have had a partner. He disappeared. A surveillance camera caught him leaving the airport with another man. The reason I bring this up is, Crocker was staying at a hotel in Pentagon City—the hotel we think was at the center of all this."

We walked for about fifteen minutes, picking our way between fallen trees, wrecked cars, pieces of houses and other buildings, and bodies. It was bad. Almost as bad as Dresden. At least nothing was on fire.

A demon rose up from behind a wrecked car, grabbed a soldier, and bit his head off. The nearest soldier raised his rifle and fired, but the demon threw the body at him and knocked him off his feet.

From the corner of my eye, I saw Isabella start to shift, but I was already moving, drawing my sword as I ran toward the demon.

Purple and muscled like a weight lifter, it was at least eight feet tall. Instead of aiming at its neck, I swung at its midsection, and my sword sliced through its abdomen. I aimed the back swing a little lower.

The demon opened its mouth and roared, reaching for me. I dove to my left, tucked, landed, and rolled to my feet. The demon took a step toward me, but when its feet tangled in its intestines, it tripped and fell. Before it could do anything else, I brought my sword down on its neck, and its head bounced away.

I leaned over, my hands on my knees, and tried to catch my breath. Isabella in jaguar form stood next to me, scanning the area for more trouble.

When I could speak, I told Torbert, "It might be safer if the soldiers just waited for us."

"I'm afraid I can't do that, ma'am," one of the soldiers said. "We have our orders." He looked around at the other soldiers and yelled, "Heads up. We're not out here for a Sunday stroll. Move out and keep your eyes open."

I felt sorry for the men, especially the man who had been knocked over by his comrade's body. The look in his eyes was one I'd seen many times in Germany during and after World War II.

The next demon we encountered was greeted with explosive ammunition by at least four of the soldiers. It kept coming after us until one of the bullets hit it in the head. I became increasingly uneasy. The demons we had seen were major demons, nasty enough to wreak havoc, but killable. Killing a greater demon usually required magic, and I hadn't seen anything from Bronski, our only mage.

Isabella hadn't shifted back, stalking along about ten feet to my left. Torbert and Wen-li kept shooting glances at her, and at least one of the soldiers was completely freaked out by her change. Her willingness to take on a demon in that form kind of freaked me out, too.

As we progressed, the damage became more severe. It looked like what I'd seen on TV of cities that were hit by a tornado or a hurricane.

"As best we can tell, this is wind damage, essentially the shock wave from the blast, Torbert said.

"You sounded skeptical when I asked you about the explosion," I said.

He shook his head. "That's because there wasn't one. At least, not an explosion in the typical sense. No sound, no smoke, no fire. Witnesses say there was a blinding flash of light, and the hotel walls simply dissolved, along with everything else for about half a mile in all directions. The pilot of a plane landing at Reagan said it looked like a wave of light expanding from the center that left nothing in its wake."

All I could do was shake my head. I had seen some impressive displays of magic in the various realms I'd traveled through, but nothing like that.

My worst fear stepped out of a ruined building and roasted the soldier nearest it with a fountain of flame. The fire demon grabbed the soldier and took a bite like it was eating a turkey leg while rushing with inhuman speed toward the next soldier in the skirmish line.

The soldier was about ten feet in front of me, and I reached the demon at the same time it reached the soldier. The soldier fired his weapon into the demon's body at point-blank range as I swung my sword across the back of the demon's legs to hamstring it. It screamed, leaning backward, and Isabella landed on its back.

The demon turned toward me and I leaped away, grabbing Torbert's shoulder and pushing him to the ground on my way past him. I felt the heat of the demon's flame behind me.

When I rolled to my feet, I saw the demon on the ground with Isabella on its back. She raised her head, demon blood dripping from her jaws, and gave a roar of triumph. The demon's skull was crushed in the same way as she killed the Werewolves in that alley the night she and I met.

Torbert's jacket was on fire, and I leaped to grab it by the collar and rip it off his body. His shirt underneath showed a scorch mark, but it hadn't burned.

Bronski had evidently cast a protection spell a little late. He was singed from his head to his feet, but he didn't seem to be injured. As far as I could tell, his spell was meant to protect only him and not anyone else. Although Wen-li looked to be unharmed, when she turned away from me, I saw that the last two feet of her beautiful hair had been burned off.

I walked over to the demon. "That can't possibly taste very good," I said to Isabella. She snarled, and then pawed at her snout. I used the cloth from Torbert's ruined jacket to wipe the ichor off her. Demon blood is extremely acidic, and I was amazed to see that she didn't seem to be affected by it. One of the soldiers handed me a canteen, and I turned it upside down, washing Isabella's mouth. Then she almost gave the soldier a heart attack, rubbing against his legs and purring like a house cat.

I didn't have to guess when we reached the edge of the magic's destruction. The ground suddenly dropped about twenty feet from a clean, straight cliff to a perfectly flat plain of dirt. I could see that the depression was a perfect circle, and as Torbert had said, about a mile wide. It looked as though that piece of Earth had been picked up and relocated. I had a feeling that was exactly what had happened. The stench of blood magic was identical to that I'd felt from Weber's car and laboratory.

"Exactly how large?" I asked.

"Eighteen hundred and twenty-four yards. A little more than a mile. That number mean anything?"

I shook my head. "Isabella might know." I turned to walk away. "Yes, that is the statue's signature. Oh, and you can tell the ICAA that they can stop worrying about Vincent Crocker."

"I don't understand," Torbert said.

"The jaguar statue is the worst of blood magic artifacts. Human sacrifice. Crocker's blood was used to fuel the spell."

By the time we got back to the main body of soldiers, police, ambulances, and all the reporters and news cameras, we had dealt with two more demons. Of the twelve soldiers who started out with us, three were dead and two more were injured. None of us were unscathed. I couldn't remember being so bruised, scraped, or singed, and I wondered if my left wrist might be broken. It certainly was swollen, and it hurt like hell.

Even Isabella, who I had begun to think was invincible, walked with a limp, unable to put much weight on her left hind leg.

Military medics took charge of the injured soldiers. A tall blonde woman in a white coat led us to an ambulance, gestured to a short stool, and told me to sit down. Then she turned her attention to Isabella.

"Shift back," the woman said to the fearsome-looking cat. Isabella gave her a surly snarl in return.

"I didn't ask your opinion," the woman said. "I'm not a veterinarian. Change your shape so I can look at that leg and see what's wrong with it. I'm not going to guess where it hurts when you can tell me."

Grumbling under her breath, Isabella changed back to human, then gasped and almost fell. Little Wen-li caught her and eased her down.

The doctor raised an eyebrow, then bent down and ran her hands down Isabella's leg. Her hands didn't get very far, as the shifter jerked and let out a short cry when the woman touched her hip.

"Your hip?" the doctor asked.

"Si. I think I dislocated it. It hurts a hell of a lot less when I'm a cat."

"Well, let's see what we can do about that," the doctor said, unbuckling Isabella's belt and pulling her pants off. That revealed a bruise covering her hip and spreading halfway down her thigh.

"Well, looks as though it popped back in the socket," the doctor said. "Drink this."

Isabella took a small bottle, sipped, and made a face. "What is this? It tastes terrible."

"I didn't ask you to like it. I said to drink it."

"Your bedside manner could use a little work," Isabella grumbled, but she drank the rest of the bottle.

The doctor grinned at her and placed both her hands on Isabella's hip and thigh. "You have any heart trouble?"

"No, why?" Isabella jerked, her back arching until only her head and heels touched the ground, then she shivered, and collapsed.

"Better?" the doctor asked.

Isabella gave her a weak nod and muttered. "Yeah. Holy shit."

The doctor turned to me and said, "Let me see that wrist."

"I'm not sure I should," I answered. "I need to know what was in that potion."

"This and that. Nothing to worry about."

My good hand shot out, grabbing her by the shoulder and squeezing. It froze her in her tracks and she winced. "No, that's not good enough. I'm close to Human, but there are some things you can tolerate that I can't."

Her eyes seemed to bulge, and she gave me the ingredient list. Nothing that would hurt me, but it would probably make me groggy, if not put me to sleep. I let go of her.

"My heart's just fine. If you can heal this wrist, I would appreciate it, but I don't need the soporific."

She nodded, then took my hand and wrist in her hands. The surge of magic that flowed into me was like an electric shock. I felt something happen in my wrist, and when she released me, I flexed it, opening and closing my fist.

"That feels great. Thank you. Do you have a card?"

She laughed, reached into her pocket and handed me a business card.

"Thank you, Doctor Evans," I said, and put it away. I was a little surprised that she was a real Human doctor in addition to being a magical healer. A good person to know.

CHAPTER 11

The sun was coming up when the FBI delivered us back to the nursery. My employees were showing up for work, and the government propaganda machine was in full swing. The only news on the radio or TV was about the meteor that hit Arlington.

The conspiracy theorists were also in full swing, contributing the event to the Russians, Taliban, space aliens, or the pagan non-Humans, depending on their particular paranoia.

I took a quick shower, put on clean clothes and went outside to find Ed. "We need to take a look at what you have scheduled today," I told him. "Anything near southwest DC or in Virginia is going to be impossible to get to."

"Do you know what happened?" he asked as we compared our schedule with a map tacked on the wall.

"They're saying a meteor," I said absently.

"No, I mean really."

With a sigh, I turned to him. "A disaster. Something magical. I don't know exactly what happened, but it wasn't a meteor. The military has troops all over the place, and every hospital in the area is overrun. I was out there, and the damage looks like a tornado, but not a natural one."

He nodded. We shifted things around to send our crews out to the opposite side of the metro area, and I took a list of clients to call and explain why we were coming early, or postponing.

With that taken care of, I retreated to the cottage. Isabella came in, sniffed the air, and said, "That smells interesting." She walked over to the coffee pot.

"What is it?"

"*Dalesh.* Not for humans." I thought a moment. Isabella wasn't human. "Check it out if you wish. It has about four times as much caffeine as coffee."

She poured herself a cup and sat at the table across from me. "Elvish?"

"Yeah. Some of the refugees from Alfheim brought seeds with them. I bought some and cultivated them in one of the greenhouses. So, what are you going to do? Go back to Colorado?"

Isabella looked surprised. "I need to find the statue. You've seen what it can do."

"Is it even in this reality anymore? Hell, is the mage who did that still alive?"

"I have to assume he is, and that the artifact is still here as well."

"And that he's still in the DC area?"

She shrugged. "I understand that my being here is an imposition. I'll find a hotel. I am very grateful for your help, Kellana. I never intended that you should be risking your life fighting demons."

While I was hoping that she would agree with my assessment, I was actually uncomfortable about assuming the threat was over. Wishing that the nightmare would end hadn't worked in Germany, or during those first months in New York when I barely scraped together enough food to keep from starving. Hell, I was a Fae. Why couldn't I ever have a Fairytale happy-ever-after?

With a sigh, I said, "I feel bad about making you sleep in a tree. Grab your stuff. I have plenty of room at my house."

She gave me a strange look. "Isn't this your home?"

"Come on."

I drove her over to my place in Georgetown, gave her a key and the passcode for the alarm system, and showed her the spare bedroom. Then I tuned the wards to admit her.

"So, why are you staying over at the nursery?" she asked.

I told her about Wilcox's leaving a note at my house, and that the wards and Fairies at the nursery made me feel more secure.

"But this is a lot more comfortable," I concluded. "And with you here, I won't feel as alone and vulnerable."

While I was showing her around the house, she pointed to a picture on the mantle of Carolyn when she was young. There was another one of the two of us together, taken about twenty years later. "A friend?"

"Carolyn. The house was her family's."

"Ah, the woman who died. She was very beautiful."

I motioned to another picture, Carolyn at her eightieth birthday. "Yes, even when she grew old. She was so full of life and love of the world. I'm always amazed at the wisdom some Humans manage in spite of their short lives."

Isabella changed the subject. "Didn't Torbert say that Crocker escaped the airport with another man?"

"Yes, and they have some video of it, I guess."

"I think we need to know who that person was."

I agreed. Pulling out my phone, I called Torbert. I suspected that he hadn't slept any more than we had, and I was right. He answered on the third ring.

"Miss Rogirsdottir?"

"Agent Torbert. How's the back?"

"Better, thank you. What can I do for you?"

Torbert gave us an address, and we drove there to find a slightly rundown office building with high security and nothing that would identify its occupants. We pressed a buzzer at the front door, identified ourselves, and waited. Five minutes later, the door buzzed. I pulled it open and we walked in to face Agent Torbert and a security guard sitting behind a desk. We signed in, pressed our fingerprints to a glass plate, and were handed visitor badges.

I wondered what they would think about my fingerprints. They didn't resemble anything Human and would match every other Elf from my clan.

We walked down a dingy hallway to a creaky elevator that took us to the third floor. We followed Torbert through a room of cubicles, then through a door into a room with a couple of computers and a large monitor mounted on the wall. He sat down, typed on a keyboard, and the monitor lit up.

A grainy surveillance video showed a sidewalk outside a building. A couple of people waited with their luggage. After about thirty seconds, two men appeared. Torbert slowed the video and zoomed in. One of them was Vincent Crocker. I didn't recognize the other man. What I did notice was that he walked very close to Crocker, and his right hand was pressed to Crocker's side.

"I think he has a gun, or some kind of weapon, in his right hand," I said.

Torbert zoomed in more, then said, "I think you're right."

I glanced at Isabella. Her attention was riveted to the screen.

"Do you know him?" I asked.

"No, but there's something very familiar about him. Not someone I've met, but someone I've seen, or maybe seen a picture of him."

"Have you sent his picture to the ICAA?" I asked. "Don't you have facial recognition software? I hear about that sort of thing on TV."

Torbert sat back. "Yes, we sent it to ICAA about an hour ago. The facial recognition software takes a long time to go through all the images we have, and that image," he motioned toward the screen, "is so poor that I don't know whether we'll get no hits, or a million hits."

Isabella and I went back to my house with the intent of getting some sleep. When we got there, I turned on the TV. By the light of day, aerial photographs of the devastation showed the lie about a meteor causing it. Nothing natural could carve out a hole so even and perfect. Not only that, but pictures of other meteor strikes—which the TV station showed—had evidence of dirt and rocks ejected from the site. In Arlington, the missing material was truly missing, along with more than fifteen thousand people.

"I wonder what their next story will be?" I asked the air.

"I'm surprised the military didn't completely clamp down on the news, flight paths, and any information about it," Isabella said.

"Hard to do in this country, especially with the internet," I said. "Fifty years ago, that's what they would have done. They tried that with the Beltane demon invasion but had to give up when a demon ate those Congressmen. Too many witnesses."

"Yeah, you're right. I'm going to bed. Wake me if that mage shows up or the sun comes up in the west."

With more than six thousand casualties crowding area hospitals, businesses destroyed, and other businesses trying to operate in spite of workers they were missing, the story did not go away. Politicians struggled to find some way of using the disaster to their advantage, or conversely to figure out how to blame it on their opponents.

I hoped that we had seen the last of the jaguar statue and its disasters, at least for a while. I assumed the mage who triggered the whole mess had to be shaken by what he'd unleashed. What I wasn't thinking about were the demons.

When I awoke the next morning, I turned on the TV while making coffee. The frantic tone of the news announcer drew my attention. I went into the sitting room and could hardly believe my ears. After dark the night before, the Pentagon was assaulted by what authorities estimated were more than one thousand demons. The battle was still going on at dawn.

While I stood there, Isabella came up behind me. "Like China," she said.

"Like Midgard, only worse."

She walked around me and peered at my face. "Like Midgard? You had demon invasions of Midgard?"

The coffee pot beeped, so I headed back to the kitchen. "Yes, Midgard is very close to Hel. Between the demons and the native goblins and trolls, not to mention Human fiefdoms constantly trying to conquer each other, Midgard was a very lively place."

I poured us each a mug of coffee. "What do you say we hit a place I know for breakfast? I have a craving for eggs Chesapeake."

"Whatever you want," Isabella said. "Is that like eggs Benedict?"

"Yeah. With crabmeat. I've been staying at the cottage, so there isn't any food in the house."

As we got in the car, Isabella said, "I've meant to ask you about your sword. Demons are notoriously difficult to kill."

I chuckled. "You know, there's a philosophical debate among Elven intellectuals as to whether demons really die. Some say that their souls return to Hel and their bodies are resurrected. No matter. It's an Elven sword, forged with magic from silver and titanium. It's virtually unbreakable, very light, and holds an edge forever. I also have an athame, a ritual knife that I use in my alchemy, forged the same way. No way that I would attempt to kill a demon with an Earthen steel sword. It would probably bounce."

We found a parking space about a block from the restaurant and strolled down the street, doing a little window shopping.

"Speaking of killing demons," I said, "I've never seen another being kill a demon without using a weapon or magic. I take it that a demigod considers a demon an equal match."

"I'm not really a demigod..." she started but trailed off when I started laughing.

"Call it what you like. I'm not going to engage in an academic debate with you." I threw my arm around her shoulders and gave her a smile. "But I was sure glad you were with me the other night."

A man leaned against a building. A beautiful,

sexy, hunk of a man. Damned near as handsome as an Elf.

"Hey, ladies, looking for a little morning recreation?" he called. Pheromones rolled off him, and his smile kindled a flame between my legs. I hadn't thought about sex in ages, but suddenly, crawling in the sack with him was the most important thing in the world.

I sketched a rune and spoke a Word.

"Hey, wait, what are you doing?" he sputtered. "You bi—" He vanished.

"What the hell?" Isabella gaped at where he had been.

"Incubus," I said. "If the veils to Hel were breached, then we should assume that a whole host of its inhabitants came over. Demons, Devils, Incubi, Succubae, Imps, Rakshasa, Oni, Yaoguai, you name it."

"But, but, what did you do?"

I noticed a sheen of sweat on her face that hadn't been there a few moments before.

"Banished it. If I was a mage, depending on how strong I was, I might be able to banish those things we fought. But the minor demons don't have the strength to resist the spell. It's easier than putting up with them."

After breakfast, I took her down by the canal and the park along the Potomac. I really needed some serenity after the shocks of the past few days, and that area was the closest I could get to nature in the city.

A lot of helicopters and airplanes flew overhead, many more than normal. When we reached the river, we saw smoke rising from the direction of the Pentagon and could hear distant explosions. As we watched, two jets dove from the sky and fired missiles at the ground.

"Are you all right?" Isabella asked.

I realized I was shaking.

"You're as pale as a ghost. Even whiter than normal."

"Perhaps this wasn't a good idea," I said, turning away and stumbling back up the path.

CHAPTER 12

Torbert called. "Miss Rogirsdottir? We have a hit on the man on the surveillance video with Vincent Crocker. Are you at your nursery?"

He showed up with Wen-li and Bronski. My office was a little tight for that many people, so I invited them into the cottage kitchen and poured lemonade for everyone.

With a grim expression, Torbert tossed a large photograph of a man on the table. Isabella gasped.

"Recognize him now?" Torbert asked. "Aleksi Nieminen."

I shrugged. It didn't mean anything to me.

"Head of ICAA," Wen-li said. "Chief Counselor is his title. The Council says he disappeared about two or three weeks ago and they don't know where he is."

"Nieminen sent Crocker to DC when the jaguar statue was first put up for auction," Bronski said. "He's said to be a very powerful mage. Supposedly a summoner and conjurer. He's led the ICAA for the past forty years and was the major proponent of coming out to the world after Beltane."

"Wonderful. The fox is guarding the henhouse," I said. "So, how does that help us?"

"I'm not entirely sure it does," Torbert said. He put a thick file on the table. "You two are the ones who said you wanted to recover the artifact. Here is a copy of everything we know about him. He's originally from Finland but has been living in Romania for at least the past fifteen years. We've put out an all-points bulletin for him. What we do know is that he hasn't taken a plane or train out of this area since the event in

Arlington."

"Do you have a record of him coming here?" I asked. "Or a record of where he's been staying?"

The look I got from Torbert wasn't kind. "No, we don't."

"So, if his teleporter is working, you won't know when he leaves, either," Isabella said with an innocent smile.

After the PCU people left, Isabella took her laptop and the dossier to my sitting room and started going through it. I went back to trying to catch up on my work. When my crews came back that evening, she was still deep into it. I figured that she was the academic type, so I let her have it.

"You haven't eaten anything since breakfast," I said as the sun started to sink behind the trees. "Are you planning on fasting until you have an epiphany?"

She looked up, and I could tell it took a little while for her eyes to focus on me. "Yeah," she said, "let's go get something to eat. And then let's go hit a couple of nightclubs."

She stood, holding a palm-sized picture of Nieminen. "He seems to have some interesting pastimes. Perhaps someone here in town has seen him."

I rolled my eyes. "Okay, so what are we doing tonight?"

"There are a bunch of clubs in a part of town called Ivy City," Isabella said. "Some of them sound like the kind of thing Nieminen likes."

Aghast, I turned to her. "Are you out of your mind?"

She chuckled. "We're tough. No one will mess with us."

"We'll end up littering the streets with bodies," I grumbled. "I hate Vampires."

Gentrification had come late to Ivy City, and the area still had its run-down rough spots. Because old warehouses could be had for cheap, a number of nightclubs had opened in the area. Some of those nightclubs were run by non-Humans—Vampires, demons, and shape shifters, mostly. But the majority of the clientele were Human.

We picked up some take-out sushi on the way. The first club we visited, Sensuous Labyrinth, had a quiet and sensuous feel, and it scared the hell out of me. The demons running the club weren't interested in blood. In private rooms, succubae and incubi drained life essence from their victims. I sensed a couple of greater demons somewhere on the premises, and what they fed on, I didn't want to know.

We didn't stay long and were headed toward the exit when a succubus stepped in front of us, hand on her hip and a sneer on her face. Several other succubae and incubi crowded around us, watching.

"What are you doing here?" she asked, obviously talking to me.

"Just slumming a bit, but we're leaving now."

"How unfortunate. I'm sure some of my regulars could give you a ride you wouldn't forget."

One of her regulars pressed against my back and butt while his hand slid around my chest. Isabella's low growl attracted the succubus's attention, but I didn't need any help.

"Oh, I'm so sorry to disappoint them," I said, lifting my athame to where the incubus holding me could see it over my shoulder. "We're sort of in a hurry, but I could come back another time. Do you have a lot of regulars who want to become eunuchs?"

The guy behind me jumped away as though I'd hit him with an electric shock. "The thing is," I told the succubus, "I have to dance to get in the mood. You do allow dancing here, don't you? I like to sing, too."

Her eyes widened, and then narrowed. Her face took on an ugly expression. "Get out."

I smiled at her and patted her on the cheek as we walked by.

"What in the hell?" Isabella asked when we were outside.

"Demons don't like the way Elves dance," I said as I headed to the car.

Isabella trotted ahead and jumped in front of me. "Oh, no, you don't. Explain."

"I was just playing on an old stereotype, that's all."

"What stereotype?"

I could see that she wasn't going to let it go. "Old tales about Elven women tell of us luring men to their doom by dancing and seducing them. We're supposed to be sirens, the ultimate in femme fatales. I guess our hostess is rather insecure. She didn't seem to like the idea of competition."

"You're joking."

I laughed. "Carolyn showed me a passage in an old book of hers. It's in the library at the townhouse. *The women of the Folk are to be avoided. When they sing and dance, no man can but go to them, but to lie with them is to surrender your soul. Their skills in the arts of love are so intense few men can survive it, and those who do pine away and die,*" I quoted. "It's very flattering, but I have a hard time reconciling it with my lack of a love life."

Isabella's expression was skeptical, but she relented.

"What I can't figure is why Nieminen would be attracted to that place," I said as we drove to the next place on our list.

"They say that sex with a succubus is addictive. We know he's pretty twisted if he's into death magic."

Vampires ran Fang, the next nightclub we visited, and they didn't try to hide it. Young Humans dressed in goth attire swarmed the place, while a death-metal band attempted to deafen everyone. The vamps didn't need to pretend, so they were dressed to impress. I hadn't seen so much glitter since I did the flowers for a kindergarten party.

I adopted a light glamour, changing my hair to black. With my pale complexion and wearing black, I fit right in. I quickly noticed dozens of small private rooms along one of the walls, and further exploration revealed more such rooms on the second floor. The smell of blood made it evident what the vampires were doing with the customers they seduced.

I felt exposed. It felt like every vampire, male and female, noticed me. Not only noticed me but followed me around. They kept whispering, "Sweet blood," which made me extremely uncomfortable.

The bartender brought me a glass of wine and stood staring at me, long after Isabella paid him, breathing deeply as though smelling me. When he finally turned away, I cast a purification spell on the wine. It flashed bright orange for an instant, confirming my suspicion that it was drugged.

Nieminen wasn't there, either. We asked one of the bouncers about him, and the guy said, "Yeah, he comes in sometimes, but I haven't seen him tonight."

"So, he's a blood whore?" Isabella asked, referring

115

to Humans who became addicted to the high they received when a Vampire fed on them.

"Naw. He's what we call a scavenger. He picks up the girls after a vamp has had them." The bouncer shrugged. "They're pretty out of it after a good ride and drain." He leered at me, then continued. "It's not like he's Prince Charming, so I guess he takes what he can get. But what the hell, everyone has their kinks, ya know? He tips well and doesn't cause any problems."

In both clubs, as far as I could tell, the management rigidly enforced a policy of limited dining. We watched a couple of college-age girls in spiked heels and tiny miniskirts teeter out and practically fall into a cab, the bruising on their necks and wrists starkly visible.

"Yeah, I guess they are out of it," I said.

"At least they still have blood in them," Isabella said. "I'm not sure they do when Nieminen gets through with them."

"So, where to?" I asked as I climbed behind the wheel of my van the following evening.

Isabella named a restaurant in the southeastern part of town. "PCU's dossier says that when Nieminen is in DC, he eats there all the time, like three out of four nights."

"Call for reservations," I said. "It sounds like we'll be fighting for a table with Torbert."

She laughed but called. When she hung up, she said, "They have a cancellation if we can get there in forty-five minutes."

Because of all the road closings, I had to take the long way around the metro area, and it took over an hour to get to the restaurant. Being late turned out not to be an issue. They had a lot of empty tables, and I wondered how many of their customers had lived in Pentagon City.

The white linen tablecloths, crystal glassware, and elegant menus gave me pause even before I saw the prices. Something must have shown on my face, because Isabella leaned forward and said, "My treat. Just order what you want. You're saving me a fortune in hotel bills."

She ordered an enormous steak intended for two people. "Rare. Just sear it on both sides," she told the waiter.

The lobster I ordered was less than half the price of her meal, so I didn't feel too bad. I tried to remember when I last ate in such a place, and the only memory that surfaced was Carolyn's last birthday. The night she handed me the deed to the townhouse in Georgetown.

"Are you okay?" Isabella asked.

I forced a smile to my face. "Yeah, I'm fine. Just a memory that made me sad for a moment."

After dinner, we approached the maître d'—a striking blonde in her thirties with 'Jennie' on the badge pinned to her blouse—and showed her the picture of Nieminen.

"Has this man been in recently?" I asked as I handed her the picture.

She froze for a moment, then said, "No, not recently. I believe it's been some time since he was here."

"So, you know him, then?"

A hesitation. "Uh, yes. He comes in sometimes. I believe he's a foreigner."

She handed back the picture, and I brushed her hand in taking it.

"Thank you," I said. "I heard he is in town, but we haven't managed to connect. I hope he wasn't caught up in that unpleasantness over in Virginia."

The woman gave me a horrified look, then tried to cover it. "Isn't that terrible?" she said.

When we got outside, Isabella said, "I don't think she was telling us the truth."

I laughed. "Humans lie about everything, but an Elf can't without harming their aura and diminishing their magic. She is some kind of witch, or maybe a low-level mage. I'm sure she has seen him recently—not only seen him, but she knows him as more than just a customer."

"If she knows who he is, and she's a magic user, then she may think of him as a kind of celebrity," Isabella said.

"She may see him as her tribal chieftain."

Isabella gave me a sideways look. "Si, maybe something like that."

"Which means she may be calling him right now, telling him about us."

"I'm sure Torbert's men have asked about him as well," Isabella said.

We parked down the street and waited. At about ten o'clock, Jennie left the restaurant, got in a car, and drove away. We followed her. She drove about thirty minutes to a residential neighborhood in a Maryland suburb, parked her car in the driveway of a house, and went inside. A couple of lights went on in the house.

We got out of the car. Isabella stood in the shadow of a tree a few houses down and across the street. I shrank down to my smaller size and sat under the woman's car. Both of us had far better night vision than a Human.

About twenty minutes later, a man in a long black hooded cloak walked down the street. I had to fight a giggle. If he was trying to look inconspicuous, that cloak wasn't the way to do it.

Jennie answered the door and let him in. I looked around but couldn't see Isabella any longer. I walked over to a place where bushes concealed me from the street, grew back to my normal size, and called her phone.

"Where are you?" I asked when she answered.

"In the alley behind the house. There are only two doors."

"What are we doing now?"

"Waiting," she said. "He doesn't have the statue with him, but maybe he'll lead us to it when he leaves."

"And how do we know he doesn't have it?"

"It weighs over three hundred pounds."

"Oh." I could carry the thing, but not easily. I couldn't see a Human carrying it at all. "I thought you said it's small."

"Gold is damned heavy."

I took her word for it. I had no idea how large three hundred pounds of gold would be. Not for the first time, I wondered why she had hooked on to me. She said she knew Elves in Colorado. Maybe I was just the dumbest Elf she could find.

An hour later, a sudden burst of magic grabbed my attention. The house I was watching took on a glow.

"Isabella, something is happening. Someone is working some potent magic in that house."

She cursed, then said, "*Santa madre.* He probably killed that poor woman."

I shuddered. "What do we do?"

"I don't know. I think we stick to our plan. We follow him when he leaves."

"If he doesn't have the statue, why would he kill her?" I asked. "Wouldn't he take her where the statue is?"

"Oh, shit," Isabella said. "He has the statue here."

"I don't feel it. I don't think it's been here. I think we should interrupt him."

Pulling my bow and quiver out of my bag, I snuck up to the house. If Nieminen was working in a protective containment area, sticking a sword into it would be stupid. But the Fairies' wooden spears had penetrated Crocker's pentagram, so I hoped I would get the same result with a wooden arrow if I fired it at Nieminen.

The blinds were closed, so I couldn't see through the window. To my surprise, the front door wasn't locked. When I cautiously pushed the door open, the force of the magic being used hit me at the same time as the smell of blood. I backed out and called Isabella.

"I think you're right," I said when she answered. "I'm going to confront him. A distraction from the rear of the house would be appreciated."

"That I can do," she said. "Be careful."

I edged back into the house, an arrow nocked. A sitting room to my right and a dining room to my left were empty. The back door crashed in, and a jaguar stood in the kitchen. She cocked her head at me, and I motioned to a door.

"I think they're in the basement," I said, going over to the door. Turning the knob, I pulled the door open. Golden light almost blinded me.

Before I could start through the door, Isabella pushed by me and flowed down the stairs, her belly brushing the treads. I followed her, my bow ready and the arrow half-drawn.

A man in black stood inside a pentagram with his back to us, and his red-stained hands raised above his head. Past him, Jennie lay naked on an altar inside a second pentagram. Her eyes were open, and her face wore a serene, almost worshipful expression as she stared up at him. Blood covered her breasts and the inside of her thighs.

The golden light pulsed, and I realized it had a pattern that matched a beating heart. That's when my view of his hands came into focus, and I realized that he held a human heart. A beating human heart.

The air shimmered past the altar, and a demon appeared, its image flickering like a bad hologram. Without thinking, I raised my bow, pulled, and loosed the arrow. I fired a second arrow even before the first bounced off the containment field. Isabella roared.

The mage whirled about, his chant faltering, and the demon faded a bit. Seeing the mage's face confirmed he was Nieminen. He was naked under the cloak and his genitals were covered in blood.

My second arrow hit the containment field, and the field flared. I pulled my athame and threw it. It passed through the field and imbedded itself in the mage's left shoulder. He screamed, dropping the heart. When it hit the floor, Jennie screamed.

The demon coalesced, staring down at the woman on the altar with an expression that combined a sexual leer with a cruel hunger. It thrust its hand into

121

Jennie's chest, pulled out red, bleeding flesh, and stuffed it in its mouth.

The two pentagrams flared red, and then dissolved. A strong wind blew into my face, and I barely had time to raise my arms and block the blow Nieminen aimed at me as he knocked me into the stair rail. And then he was past me, rushing up the stairs.

Isabella and I had a larger problem than the mage. She leaped to the side, and the demon's swipe with its four-inch claws narrowly missed her. I fired an arrow, which almost found its target, cutting a bloody line along the side of the demon's head, less than half an inch from its eye.

I drew my sword and braced myself as the demon lunged toward me. Its hands reached out to me, but I leapt forward, and my sword found its mark, plunging through the demon's left eye and into its brain.

It tried to grasp me in a bear hug, but I dropped to the floor and shrunk to avoid it. I slipped between the demon's legs even as Isabella landed on its back and bit its head. Growing back to my normal size, I watched her ride it to the floor.

Pulling my sword out of the demon's brain, I raised it in both hands, and brought it down, cutting off its head. The head bounced away and landed upright on its neck. It grinned at me, sticking its tongue out and licking its lips. It laughed, then both the head and its body faded, leaving only a few gallons of demon blood to prove it hadn't been an illusion.

Jennie's heart lay on the floor, its beat slowing. I watched her face, and she watched me. When her heart stopped beating, I saw the light go out in her eyes.

CHAPTER 13

We sat outside while we waited for Torbert and the local police. The locals got there first. Isabella, of course, looked as pristine as she did when we left home. Damned shape shifter.

I, on the other hand, needed a brush. And some fresh clothes. My shirt hung in charred tatters with red flesh and blisters showing through the holes. Though I hadn't seen any flames, there certainly was evidence of a great amount of heat. The mage felt like he was on fire when he ran into me. Then there was the demon blood, which had eaten holes in the shirt, my jeans, and my boots.

At least I had recovered my athame. I found it lying in a large pool of blood on the floor by the front door. Damned fool should have known better than to pull the knife out.

The first two cops pulled up, glanced at us, then entered the open door of the house. We heard them search through the main floor, and then go down to the basement. We could hear their cautious descent, then the pounding of their feet as they rushed up the stairs and back outside where they threw up.

The next people on the scene were a couple of detectives. After they surveyed the basement, one of them drew Isabella away to talk to her, and the other squatted down in front of where I sat on the steps.

"What's your name, Miss?"

"Kellana Rogirsdottir." I spelled it out for him.

"What happened here?"

"We interrupted a sacrifice, but we were too late."

He chewed on his pencil, then asked, "How did you know there was a sacrifice?"

I shook my head. "We didn't."

The detective didn't seem too pleased with the volume of information I was dispensing. What was I supposed to tell him? That we were following a blood mage hoping to prevent the next near-nuclear catastrophe?

By the time Torbert showed up, there were a dozen cops, an ambulance, forensics people, and a medical examiner traipsing around, and most of the neighbors were awake and providing an audience beyond the yellow tape. It looked like a scene from a TV show.

Torbert talked with the detective for a while, then wandered over to the curb where the cops had us sit.

"Are you all right?" he asked me, bending close.

"I don't know," Isabella said. "She refuses to answer that question."

"I just want to go home."

He reached out and moved my arm. It took me by surprise when he touched one of my burns, and I snarled at him. His eyes widened, then he took a step back, straightened, and waved to someone.

Two paramedics came over, and the woman squatted in front of me. "Let me see," she said

I opened my arms and let her see my ruined shirt, and what it showed of my wounds underneath it. She sucked air through her teeth, and I heard a soft gasp from Torbert.

"She needs a hospital," the paramedic told Torbert.

"I need to go home."

124

"Doesn't that hurt?" the male paramedic asked.

"It hurts like bloody hell. I have medicine at home."

"I don't think…" he started to say, but I stood up, and his voice tailed off as his eyes followed me upward.

"Am I under arrest, Agent Torbert?"

"No, of course not. We have a lot of questions, though."

"You can ask them tomorrow. Isabella, can you get the keys out of my pocket?" While she pulled out my keys, I told Torbert, "The blood upstairs is Nieminen's. You want to collect it because it can be used to trace him."

I ignored Torbert, the detective, and the paramedics, who all called after us as we walked away.

As she started the car, Isabella asked, "Are you going to be all right?"

"I think so. It's all just surface burns."

When we got home, Isabella helped me peel my clothes off, and then took the pot of burn ointment and spread it on me. My mother was an apothecary, and though my magic wasn't as strong as hers, I was competent enough to prepare basic medicines.

The cooling effect of the ointment was immediate, and as more and more of the burned area was covered, I felt the tension and pain flow out of me.

"You're lucky," Isabella said as she worked. "All the burns are on your front. You'll be able to sleep on your back."

I didn't feel particularly lucky.

"We did solve one mystery tonight," Isabella said.

"Nieminen was the man I smelled at Weber's house. He was the murderer."

Torbert showed up with Wen-li and Bronski the following morning, just as the last of my crews pulled out of the compound. I invited them into the cottage and put on another pot of coffee.

"You look a lot better than you did last night," Torbert said.

"I'm still a bit tender."

"So, what happened?" he asked.

I nodded to Isabella, who told them about Nieminen, Jennie, and the demon while I poured coffee for everyone.

When she finished, Torbert said, "Her name was Jennifer Watkins, age thirty-six, divorced, no children. She owned the house."

"You said there was a demon," Wen-li interjected. "We found demon blood, but what happened to the demon itself. Did it escape?"

Isabella looked to me.

"It was a major demon, an old one. We killed it, cut off its head, and then it laughed at us and disappeared."

I gave them a little time to digest that.

"Some legends say that major demons are immortal. You can put them in a blender, but they reincorporate." I shrugged. "I've never studied demons, and that's the strongest major demon I've encountered, so I'm not an expert. I saw a greater demon when I was young, but a mage fought it. My mother wouldn't let me watch the battle, so I don't know what happened to it."

Bronski was usually very quiet, but he pursed his lips and said, "Dave told us that you said we can trace Nieminen using his blood. I'm not familiar with blood magic. Is this something you can do?"

My respect for his magical skills dropped even lower. I wondered if the man had ever studied his craft.

"It's not blood magic. I was referring to a simple tracking spell. Hair, fingernail clippings, anything that was physically a part of him would work, but blood works the best. I'm sure any competent magic user could do it."

As they were leaving, I drew Wen-li aside. "I know that Bronski has magic," I said, "but I'm astonished that he didn't know what a tracking spell is."

She bit her lip and glanced in his direction. "Yeah. Kind of strange." She didn't say anything else, but I could see concern in her face.

I went back inside the cottage, where Isabella had cleared the table and was washing the dishes. My shirt irritated my burns, so I took it off, poured a glass of lemonade, and sat in front of the air conditioner.

"I can't believe that you jumped on a fire demon and didn't even singe your whiskers," I said. "Must be nice to be a demigod."

Isabella smirked. "Demigod is not exactly correct."

"Not fair," I grumbled.

"Some people are born with great beauty, others get immunity to fire demons. Life is fair in its own way," she said.

Not feeling particularly philosophical that morning, I said, "I don't trust Agent Bronski."

"Which proves that you're a good judge of

character," Isabella said. "I wonder how long he's been working with the PCU."

I gave her a raised eyebrow look and waited for her to clarify. In response, she chuckled, then said, "It might be interesting to find out if he volunteered to work with them before or after Weber put the statue up for auction."

After cleaning up, Isabella announced that she was going grocery shopping, an activity she had shown little interest in during the time I had known her. She was usually happy with giving me money and eating any large slabs of meat I might bring home.

"Is there anything in particular you want me to pick up?" she asked as she started out the door.

"Ten pounds of beet roots."

She stopped. "Got a major craving for beets?"

I shook my head. "I need to get smart about fighting demons. This charging-into battle-waving-a-sword business is stupid. I'm not a battle mage. Hell, I'm not even a particularly strong hedge witch. But I am a trained alchemist. Demonbane. I can cook up some demonbane, fill some paintballs with it, and shoot them from beyond arm's reach."

Isabella wasn't easily impressed, but the look on her face showed that what I said impressed her. Whether with my idea, or my stupidity at taking so long to figure it out, I didn't want to ask.

"There's such a thing as demonbane?"

"Sure. You've seen those reddish-purple pillars surrounding the Capitol and the White House?" I asked.

She nodded.

"Limestone coated in demonbane," I said. "Either they found an Elf to make it for them, or a human magician cooked up something comparable."

"So, you make demonbane from beets? I mean, I'm half demon, and though beets aren't my favorite, I've eaten them."

I chuckled. "It's one of the ingredients. Cinnabar, mandrake root, and torbernite in a beet juice solution. Since we have some demon blood, we'll use that as well. Add a bit of magic to bind it all together, and you get a solution so toxic that even demons can't stand it."

"I'm not familiar with all that stuff," she said.

"Cinnabar is mercury sulfide. You can't even handle it with your bare hands. Torbernite is found here on Earth, but it's much more common in Hel. It's a crystal formed from phosphorous, copper, water and uranium. Mandrake root contains hallucinogenic neurotoxins."

"Sounds nasty. Where do the beets come in?"

"Demons hate beets. You can use carrots if you don't have beets, but they don't work as well."

She pursed her mouth and stared at me, then said in a dry voice, "Anything else you need?"

"A bottle of nice red wine and some dark chocolate."

Isabella rolled her eyes and walked out.

CHAPTER 14

Isabella surprised me by bringing home some food besides meat, then shocked me by cooking shrimp fajitas with onions, spicy peppers, and tomatoes, served with guacamole and refried beans.

"You need to recover your strength," she told me as she set the feast on the table.

"Where did you learn to cook?" I asked. The exotic smells almost had me drooling.

"I've lived a long time," she said, "and I've picked up a few skills along the way. Acceptance of the existence of non-Humans is still sketchy, and I don't think most people are ready for beings such as me."

I nodded as I chewed grilled shrimp and swallowed. "Most people are willing to accept me as a witch, whether they believe I have any magic or not. You know, sort of like they would accept me as a Presbyterian. But to tell them I'm an Elf? Someone not born on this planet, and fundamentally, biologically different than they are? No, they have a problem with that."

"But you're not biologically different. Elves can interbreed with Humans."

"And Angels, and Devils, and some say the Aesir and Giants, though I won't be testing that last one. I guess you might call all of us subspecies. But crossbreeds have limitations. Donkeys and horses can interbreed, but their offspring are sterile. A Human-Elf child will be a witch, but his or her magic will be different from either parent. A Nephilim who is half Elf is very different from one who is half Human. Did you know that a half-Elf Nephilim and a half-Human Nephilim can't produce viable children? The issue is always miscarried."

"I guess you saw a lot on your journey to get here," Isabella said, a wistful note in her voice.

"Some places I would like to visit again, some I hope I never do. A couple where I might choose to live if I had a choice. Earth is a very violent and cruel place. It's not like that everywhere."

"And Midgard?"

"Better than Earth, I think. Still filled with war and strife, ambition, intolerance and greed." I smiled. "But I haven't seen all the realms, only half. Maybe someday I'll snag myself another handsome realm walker."

Isabella insisted on doing the dishes, so I washed and trimmed the beets and took them down to my lab. I was busy lining up ingredients for the demonbane when she came in and stood in the doorway.

"Wow. I don't know what I expected when you said a lab, but this looks like a modern chemistry laboratory."

"Carolyn modernized it. My lab at the cottage is a lot more rustic. In addition to being a witch, an apothecary and an alchemist, she was a licensed pharmacist. A very smart and talented woman. I learned a lot from her."

"And you still miss her."

"Oh, yes. She was my best friend for fifty years. We lived together for the last thirty years of her life. I still catch myself expecting her to be here. When you came back from the store tonight, it was kind of a shock to hear your voice. Your mind falls into patterns, and for thirty years, the someone else walking in the door was always Carolyn."

Isabella might have heard something in my voice,

because she changed the subject. "You said the ingredients in this demonbane are highly toxic in themselves. You keep that sort of thing around?"

I chuckled and picked up my grimoire. Walking over to her, I turned to a page near the back of the book.

"You won't be able to read this, but this is a list of minerals," I paged through the section showing her, "with pictures, descriptions, and references. There are sections for plants and animals and other things. The landscaping business is pretty slow in the winter, so I travel and collect things. Especially rare things, such as torbernite, that I can't get at the market."

Wearing doubled surgical gloves, I transferred all the ingredients to the glovebox under the vent hood. "I learned by casting wards around workings such as this, but adding a second level of safety is great. Now, as soon as the beet juice cooks down, I'll be ready to go."

Concocting the demonbane took about three hours, but came off without a hitch, even though I'd never made it before. The final product turned out to be far more radioactive than the torbernite, which made me uneasy. The next step was to fill paintballs with it. The stuff turned out to be more corrosive than I expected and it melted the plastic balls I injected it into.

"Not good?" Isabella asked.

"Not good."

I searched through both my book and Carolyn's before finding a possible solution on Google. Some years before, I had bought two cases of lead crystal glasses from an estate sale, and they still sat in their boxes in the attic.

I put a glass between two metal plates, and using

magic to supply the needed weight, ground it into powder. I had molds for paintballs, because I often made them with solid substances. First, I poured the demonbane liquid into the molds, then I sprinkled a layer of glass over each one. Sketching three runes into the air, I spoke a Word. There was a flash of light, and I had thirty-two purple balls. Ta-da!

The Geiger counter stayed quiet when I scanned them, and when I put one under the spectrometer, it gave me the boring reading of leaded glass.

"Fantastic!" I jumped up and down and clapped my hands like a little girl.

"I take it that it worked? What was destroying that beautiful glass all about?"

I picked up one of the balls and handed it to her. "The demonbane is acidic, so I needed glass to contain it. It's also radioactive, so the leaded glass blocks that. The magic spell created a ball of glass and sucked the liquid inside. Be careful with them. By necessity, the glass is fragile, so that it shatters easily when it hits a demon."

"And this will kill a demon?"

I shrugged. "Maybe. If all it does is chase them away, I'll be happy." I showed her my paintball gun and filled the hopper with the balls. "I bought it for vampires. They were a real problem a couple of years ago, right after the breach. More vampires than rats in DC."

"That's genius!"

"Well, I can't take credit for the idea. I read it in a fiction novel about a witch who filled paintballs with potions."

Torbert came by the nursery the following morning. "Just thought I'd stop by and check on you. Have you had any new lurkers or mages trying to break in?"

"Things have been rather dull since Nieminen blew up Virginia," I said. "Any luck on tracking him down?"

"We checked every hospital and clinic in the metro area and didn't get a hit. Maybe he wasn't hurt as badly as you thought."

Isabella snorted. "He was bleeding like a stuck pig." She shook her head. "He's the head of ICAA. Did you bother to ask ICAA for a list of their registered healers in the area?"

Torbert stared at her, then blinked and said, "You must think I'm the dumbest person in the world. No, we didn't."

He whipped out his phone and made a call, wandering away from us as he talked. Isabella and I exchanged an eye roll. It wasn't as though Torbert didn't know about magical healing—he employed a healer—but he still tried to view paranormal actions through a familiar lens.

Torbert shouted in alarm, and I turned back to see what the problem was. I saw him stumbling backward, then he fell on his butt. I ran over to where he sat, looking around for some sign of trouble. I didn't spot anything except Fred, standing a few feet from the open door of his house, staring at Torbert.

"What's wrong?" I asked, while extending a hand to help him up.

"What is that?" he asked, pointing to Fred.

"That's Fred. He lives here."

Gnomes are humanoid, one to two feet tall, but

134

with gray skin, hair that resembles dried grass, and features that look like a withered potato. They aren't most Elves' idea of attractive. Probably not attractive to Humans, either.

Torbert gave me a kind of wide-eyed look, so I figured I needed to explain a little more. "He's a Gnome. He does most of my pest control and all the irrigation. He and his wife, Kate, live under that mound over there."

"He just emerged out of solid ground!"

"Well, yeah. He does that. Gnomes move through earth like fish swim through water. That's what makes him so good at laying irrigation lines. We don't have to dig."

I pulled Torbert to his feet. Then I walked over to Fred, calmed him down, and assured him that the big man wouldn't yell at him anymore.

Taking Torbert by the arm, I pulled him toward the cottage. "Let's go talk somewhere more private. You about scared the poor Gnome half to death."

"I scared him?"

"Yes, you're large, loud, and you don't belong here. You startled him."

I brewed a relaxation tea of lemon balm and lavender, poured it over ice, and gave a glass to Torbert. "Here, drink this. You know, in your line of work, you really need to react better to beings you haven't seen before."

Isabella sniggered and poured herself some tea.

"I know you have witches and mages working for you," I said. "Don't you have any non-Humans? I mean, it never would have occurred to me to go to a Human hospital. Goddess knows what kind of superstitious mumbo jumbo they practice in those places."

Torbert choked on his tea, and when he finished coughing, I smiled and winked at him.

"Seriously, though," Isabella said. "In spite of his high-sounding position at ICAA, Nieminen, like most of us, has spent his life hiding in the shadows. He isn't going to be easy to catch. You're going to have to enlist the paranormal community."

CHAPTER 15

We went to the shopping district of Georgetown for dinner and then planned on going to a pub with Irish music. We didn't quite make it to the pub. It was almost dark when a tiny woman with black hair, who stood barely as tall as my waist, intercepted us on the street.

"I wish to speak with you about a statue," she said in accented English.

"Which statue are you looking for?" I asked, assuming she was a Japanese tourist.

"The jaguar statue, of course."

I felt Isabella move a little away from me, giving both of us more freedom of movement.

"May I know your name?" I asked, my left hand falling into my bag and gripping my athame.

"Akari Nakamura," she said with a bow. "Harold Vance told me I should speak with you."

"I see. Was he hoping you would kill me, or that I would kill you?"

Isabella choked, and the woman standing in front of me fought very hard to keep a straight face.

"Possibly both," she said. "He didn't specify."

"I'm afraid I can't help you. I don't know where it is."

She studied my face, as though trying to tell if I was lying. "Do you know who has it?"

"I wouldn't help you find it if I did."

"I see. I am willing to pay quite handsomely for information," Nakamura said.

"Have you ever been to Arlington, Virginia?" I

asked. "Perhaps you can find some clue there."

"Incoming," Isabella shouted.

I looked toward where she was standing next to the railing overlooking the canal. Or rather, where she had been standing. She was backpedaling and starting to shift. Crawling over the rail were a pair of demons. A quick glance over my shoulder showed two more coming up from the canal on the other side of the street.

"Friends of yours?" I asked Nakamura as I drew my sword. With my other hand, I pulled out my paintball gun and fired at the closest demon across the street. My first shot caused a purple splash on its abdomen, the next two paintballs hit its chest and face. With the last shot, it stopped, its hands went to its face, and it let out a scream that might have been heard for miles. The other one paused to grab an unlucky pedestrian and take a bite.

The tiny woman turned to face the demon while she chanted a spell in a sing-song language I didn't understand. I spun and saw two demons flanking Isabella, who had completed her shift. I shot the closest demon, hitting it in the thigh. It made a screeching sound and grabbed at its leg, then cried out again, shaking its hand away from its body.

Isabella danced around the other one, but I couldn't get a shot at it for fear of hitting her. Glancing back at the demons across the road, I saw the first demon rolling around and screeching, as though in agony. Its skin had turned beet-purple-red and was flaking away. The second demon was frozen in place. The diminutive mage continued to chant, her hands held above her head. Just to be on the safe side, I shot the demon she had immobilized.

Whatever spell she had used to stop the demon

didn't stop my paintball. Beet-red liquid splashed across the creature's arm and torso.

The demon I had crippled with the thigh shot offered no resistance to me walking up and cutting off its head with my sword, so I did. The last demon was turned away from me, trying to catch Isabella. I rushed toward it and hamstrung first one leg, then the other, and it fell to its knees. That gave the jaguar all the opening she needed as she leaped into the air, landed on the demon's back, and crushed its skull with her powerful jaws.

Nakamura stopped chanting, and I whipped around to see her standing with her hands at her sides, watching the two demons I had shot. They appeared to be dying, flailing around in the street but growing weaker. The first one's skin had about flaked away, and the flesh beneath it seemed to be turning mushy. Its cries became progressively weaker.

The mage's eyes were wide as she said, "What is that stuff?"

"Demonbane."

"Not like any demonbane I ever heard of. That is potent shit."

I shrugged. "First time I ever used it. I didn't think it would kill them."

Isabella walked stiff-legged to where we stood. I could tell by her posture that she was extremely wary of our new companion.

Nakamura reached out and ran her hand down Isabella's back, eliciting a growl from the big cat.

"So soft," Nakamura said.

We ended up at a coffeeshop instead of the Irish pub. Nakamura insisted that she wanted the jaguar statue only to keep it out of the hands of blood mages and that she had the power to keep it safe and hidden.

I could tell that Isabella wasn't buying any of it. After seeing the crater in Arlington, I was inclined toward doubting that anything in Earth's realm was capable of containing the statue's power. Whether we believed Nakamura or not, we didn't have the artifact. She wasn't happy, but we parted on cordial terms. Nakamura said that she would tap into her network of acquaintances in hopes of hearing news of Nieminen.

As we walked home, Isabella said, "I wonder if Nieminen might have felt the same way before he actually touched the thing."

"Do you mean he just wanted to shield the world from the statue's power, but it corrupted him?"

"Exactly. It was created by a blood mage seeking great power, and then consecrated over and over by blood mages who were demigods. Whatever their motivations, the religion of the Mesoamerican civilizations from the Olmecs through the Aztecs were bloody abominations. The statue is the center of all that and its legacy."

"So," I said, watching her face carefully, "what makes you think that you won't want all that power for yourself?"

She laughed. "I don't have any magic, remember? I can't feel the thing, wouldn't have any idea how to use it."

"So you say. You *are* magic. You said yourself that you have certain powers from your parents."

Isabella sobered and stopped, turning to face me. "The powers I am able to wield are not innate. They are not part of me. I can call on my mother and channel her power through me. But I am not a god. How much of her power I can withstand is finite. In more than a thousand years, I have called such power

140

fewer times than I can count on one hand. Do you understand what I'm saying?"

I understood the difference between magic and the powers of a god. Elves understood such things because our goddess often walked among us. Although I had never met Danu, my mother had, and I believed her.

"Yes, I understand."

We continued walking, and after a short while, Isabella said, "I think I'll buy a paintball gun tomorrow."

When we got home, I pulled out a bottle of wine and some chocolate. Then I put an Irish music CD on the stereo.

"We don't seem to ever make it to the pub, do we?" Isabella said, taking the glass I poured for her.

"I used to make it there almost every week. Then one night I ran into a jaguar shifter, and my whole life turned upside down."

"Sorry."

"No, you're not, but that's okay." I sat in my favorite chair and got comfortable. I would have loved a fire in the fireplace, but that would have been crazy in DC in June. "What do you make of our new friend?"

"Akari Nakamura?" Isabella gave me a sardonic grin. "She's another one of the professors you're so fond of. Professor of Archeology at Nagoya University in Japan. I looked her up on Google. At one time, she also sat on the ICAA, but gave up her seat a couple of decades ago. So, she knows Nieminen very well."

Isabella took a sip of her wine and cast a glance at the fireplace. Evidently, she felt the same way about it as I did.

"You didn't seem surprised when she told you Harold Vance sent her," she said.

"She was one of the buyers who hired Vance and his Werewolves to find the statue. He said she offered two-and-a-half million dollars for it. But that attack tonight was a little too convenient. Four demons attacking us on that bridge at the same time she approaches us? I think she planned to be our savior."

"Makes sense. I thought demons don't like running water."

"They don't. I can't imagine them choosing to hang over it so they could ambush us on a bridge. Actually, I can't imagine a bunch of demons ambushing us at all, unless someone directed them to. They could have had a far better meal two blocks up the street."

CHAPTER 16

Word of Nieminen came not from Torbert or Nakamura but from an unexpected source. Abner Wilcox knocked on the door of my townhouse one evening while we were cooking dinner.

Puzzled at who might be knocking, I looked out the window.

"Isabella, it's that Abner Wilcox mage. What do you think I should do?"

She came into the living room and peeked out. "I don't know. Can you cast one of those ward thingies to keep him out while we find out what he wants?"

I had to smile. "The ward thingies are there all the time. I just made an exception for you."

"Oh. Well, let's see what he wants."

I opened the door. "Mr. Wilcox. What an unexpected surprise."

"Doctor Wilcox," he grumbled. "I have some news you might be interested in. May I come in?"

"Well, that's rather problematic," I said. "You were quite rude the last time we met. I generally don't welcome rude people into my home."

He had the grace to blush. "I heard that Aleksi Nieminen might have the statue, and that he might have something to do with the event in Arlington."

"And?" I asked, making no move to open the screen door or allow him through the wards.

He looked up at me and said, "I think I can figure out how to find him, but I'm not up to the task of confronting him. He can't be allowed to use that abomination again. I had hoped that you and Dr. Cortez felt the same way."

"Why the change in attitude?" Isabella asked from behind me. "The last time we saw you, you were prepared to do almost anything to acquire the artifact for yourself. You attacked us."

"I wouldn't have harmed you. I simply meant—"

I cut him off. "You simply meant to make us your prisoners and force us to tell you where the statue was. I'm a very simple woman, Dr. Wilcox. There are good people, and there are bad people. I know Humans believe that good people sometimes do bad things. I know Humans believe that sometimes a lie serves a good purpose. I do not believe such things. I shall accept your help to find the statue, but do not delude yourself that I will ever trust you. Do we understand each other?"

Wilcox stared at me with his mouth hanging open. When he didn't say anything, I started to shut the door.

"Wait! Okay. All right. Whatever you say. I need your help. We need to stop Aleksi."

I nodded. "Go around to the back gate on the side." I shut the door and locked it.

"You are a hard woman," Isabella said.

"I'm an Elf. I think you will find few Elves who would disagree with what I said, and none of them will be welcome in Elven society. We don't believe in situational ethics or sliding-scale morality." I shook my head. "I can't even wrap my mind around such concepts. It constantly reminds me of how alien Humans actually are."

"But you said there is war in Alfheim," Isabella said, her brow wrinkled in puzzlement.

"Yes. There are dishonorable people who have done dishonorable things. Eventually, they will be defeated." Or at least, I fervently hoped so. Elves were as susceptible to greed, cruelty and a hunger for power as other races were. We could be devious and deceptive, but I didn't think I needed to lay out all the faults of my race to a Human. The depth of Human depravity went far beyond what the higher races could ever tolerate.

"If you will go out to the back yard and let Dr. Wilcox in the back gate, I'll finish dinner and bring it out," I said as I walked back to the kitchen. "But I refuse to let him in my house."

A small round picnic table sat in the courtyard behind my house. I loved sitting out there in the evenings, especially in the spring and autumn when the weather was nice. Although the courtyard was inside my wards, I didn't feel as though it was actually inside my home, so I could tolerate Wilcox there.

After arguing with myself for a few minutes, I found I could not bring myself to be rude even to such a loathsome Human as Wilcox. I took a bottle of wine and three glasses out to the courtyard and asked, "Are there any foods you cannot eat?"

He looked surprised. "No, I don't think so."

Since all the food I had prepared was from normal Earth sources, I assumed he could eat it. I went back to the kitchen, dished up three bowls of food, took them outside, and sat to eat. Isabella immediately began to devour her meal, but Wilcox simply stared at the food and wine as though he faced a snake.

"Are you not hungry?" I asked. I couldn't see anything that was objectionable, merely stir-fried chicken and vegetables over buckwheat with an Elven sauce. And while it wasn't the finest wine in the world, I thought it was perfectly acceptable for the price.

"Uh, I think I'll pass," Wilcox said.

Isabella glanced at him, then I saw a grin spread across her face. "He's afraid that you're going to enchant him," she said.

"It's just food we bought from the market. Why would I cast a spell on it?"

She laughed. "Ancient Earth myths. Beware of eating the Fairy food or drinking the Fairy wine. Afraid of falling under the thrall of an Elven maiden, Abner?"

He blushed bright red, which told me she was correct.

"I don't like you," I said. "Why would I want to keep you?" I stood and reached for his bowl. "No need to let food go to waste."

I was too slow. Isabella grabbed the bowl before I could and dumped the contents on top of that in her own bowl. "Save me from going for seconds," she said.

The look on Wilcox's face was priceless.

"So," Isabella said between bites, "what is this information you have on Aleksi Nieminen?"

"He was evidently hurt and went to a healer a friend of mine knows. The healer didn't know that Aleksi was wanted by the Council."

"Is he wanted by the Council?" Isabella asked. "They aren't being very cooperative with the PCU."

Wilcox snorted softly. "Do you blame them? The PCU is basically an organization to protect the untalented from the talented."

"Have you been out to Arlington, Doctor?" I asked.

"Well, I've seen pictures. The security forces won't let anyone near the place."

I polished off the last of my dinner, washed it down with some wine, and said, "We have been there.

I stood on the edge of that crater, and what I saw scared me worse than almost anything I've seen in my life. The media keeps calling it an explosion. I'm telling you that is a lie. A chunk of this reality, over a mile wide, is gone, transported somewhere else."

He took a deep breath, then a drink of his wine. "I was afraid of that," he finally said. "The authorities are trying to pass it off as a meteor, but I keep wondering where the contents of that hole disappeared to."

Shaking my head, I said, "I truly try not to think about that too much. I just hope where it landed wasn't inhabited."

I collected the dishes and took them back into the house. When I came back outside, I poured more wine all around.

"How do we find this healer?" I asked.

Wilcox's friend lived on the banks of the Chesapeake, east of DC and south of Annapolis. I drove out there with Wilcox sitting in the front seat and providing directions. Isabella sat behind him.

He said the mage we planned to meet was the long-time liaison between ICAA and the shadowy group who served in a de facto regulatory fashion over mages and witches in the United States. Wilcox professed to know him well, and said he was entirely trustworthy.

The fact that he told me that made me concerned about a trap. In my experience, as soon as a Human sought to assure me of his honesty, I could wager money he was lying. I called Torbert, but he didn't answer his cell phone. I called his office, and Wen-li answered.

"Dave is out of the office this week," she said.

"Can I help you?" I told her where we were going and who we planned to meet.

We drove toward Chesapeake Bay, eventually leaving the highway and traveling along winding back roads. At one point, I wondered if Wilcox was purposely trying to confuse me so that I didn't know where I was. If so, he had chosen a member of the wrong race. Elves don't get lost, our connection with the earth means we always know where we are.

A final turn down a narrow driveway brought us to a large house near the water. A middle-aged woman with short, light brown hair answered the door and led us to a room full of windows and an incredible view of the bay beyond.

Lord James Campbell, Earl of March, turned out to be a Scotsman with a brogue that I found a bit difficult to understand. I still had trouble determining Humans' ages, and mages were especially long lived. Campbell had white hair, a thin, stooped frame, and difficulty in walking with a cane. But his eyes were bright, and his deep baritone voice was steady as he introduced himself.

Power radiated from him. I surreptitiously sketched a rune with one hand held under the table. All I would need to do is speak the Word to invoke the spell to protect Isabella and me.

The woman who had answered the door brought in a tray with tea and biscuits, set it on the table, and retreated to the door, where she stood like a guard. She didn't look like a guard though, in her blue cotton dress with small yellow flowers. She looked like a housekeeper, although I was aware that women in such positions were often fiercely protective of their domains.

"I understand that you have some questions

concerning Aleksi Nieminen," Campbell said.

I looked to Isabella. The search was her concern, not mine.

"We are looking for him," she said.

"That doesn't provide me with any incentive to give you any information," Campbell returned.

Isabella looked back to me, so I said, "A man named Vincent Crocker attempted to breach my wards and break into my property. When he was captured, the Pontificium Consilium de Artium Arcanum Mortis stepped in and demanded his release. The Federal Paranormal Crimes Unit decided to deport him and took him to Reagan International."

I raised an eyebrow to indicate that the story was hers again.

"Crocker gave the feds the slip," Isabella said, "and a surveillance camera caught him leaving the airport with a man who was identified as Nieminen."

"Vincent Crocker is an employee of the Council," Campbell said. "I was the one who interceded with your government to have him released."

His answer seemed to irritate Isabella and Wilcox. I had to suppress a grin. Campbell would have done well negotiating with Elves.

"Have you seen the crater in Arlington?" I asked.

"I have seen pictures of it. Considering the security issues and my mobility problems, journeying to the site would be problematic."

Looking Campbell directly in the eyes, I said, "An artifact was at the site. Its imprint was unmistakable. Also unmistakable was the smell of Vincent Crocker's blood, which fueled the spell. Considering that he was last seen with Aleksi Nieminen, I think it is natural that a number of people wish to speak with him."

He regarded me for some time, then asked, "What is the nature of this artifact?"

"A golden jaguar," Isabella said, "that was removed from an ancient temple in Yucatan."

"And you think this artifact is powerful enough to blow mile-wide holes in a city?"

"Do you know of any mages powerful enough to blow mile-wide holes in a city without some kind of augmentation or help?" I asked.

He shot me a look, then sighed and relaxed back into his chair. "No, I don't. I take it that you don't consider such power as being commonplace any more than I do."

I tried to choke back the laughter that bubbled up but wasn't successful. "No, my lord, I don't." Managing to regain my composure, I said, "Perhaps a full circle of battle mages might contrive such a spell, but when I stood on the edge of the crater, I could think only of a god or an archdemon. The magical residue was far beyond anything I could have imagined, and it stank of evil."

Campbell nodded. "I don't suppose you have any insight into the origin of this artifact?"

"Are you familiar with Mesoamerican lore?" Isabella asked.

Campbell shook his head.

"Then I will simply say that it was used in blood sacrifices to call the jaguar goddess and the bat demon in rituals to affirm the ascension of a line of mage kings. It opened portals to the upper realms."

"And it was used for how long?"

"Several hundred years."

"A couple of nights ago," I said, "we interrupted Nieminen while he was cutting the heart out of a woman named Jennifer Watkins. The major demon he called was quite impressive, but fortunately we intervened before he could bind the demon. We were told that you have knowledge of him visiting a healer. We assume that was to heal a knife wound."

For the first time Campbell showed signs of agitation. He shifted in his chair, his eyes darting from me to Isabella to Wilcox and back to me again.

"I never heard of a demon using a weapon."

"It didn't. I stabbed Nieminen, and then killed the demon. It was sort of a natural progression, but Nieminen escaped."

A crashing sound from the front of the house caused everyone but Campbell to leap to their feet. But it captured even his attention. His housekeeper rushed forward, but I grabbed her arm as she passed me.

"We seem to attract demons," I said. "If you're not up for dealing with them by yourself, I would suggest staying here."

I waved my arm in a wide circle and said the Word, setting a ward on the room, then turned back to Campbell. "Is there a good escape route, my lord?"

"You think you were followed here?" he asked, evidencing little alarm and no urgency.

"I would consider it a good possibility," Isabella said. "As Kellana said, we do attract demons, which is suspicious since I hadn't seen a demon in centuries before I started hunting for the jaguar."

"Well, I am fairly confident they cannot get through my wards," Campbell said. "I would suspect the noise you're hearing is due to the demise of your vehicle."

That wasn't very reassuring. I couldn't decide if I

was glad we didn't use Isabella's rental car, or sorry that we had used mine. Dealing with the insurance company did not promise to be any fun.

A massive wave of magic swept over us, and I saw Campbell flinch. Since we weren't all immediately incinerated, I assumed his wards were holding. How much longer they would do so was the question.

"Just for the record," I said, "I would guess that was an enhanced attack. Are you still confident in your wards, my lord?"

Isabella looked out the windows toward the bay. "Do you have a boat?"

"There is a motor launch. Mary used it to fetch groceries just yesterday."

Without any hesitation, Isabella grabbed the woman's arm and pulled her toward the back door. "I assume you're Mary," she said. "Where's the boat?"

"I'm afraid I'm not as spry as I used to be," Campbell said, struggling to stand.

I scooped him into my arms even as another magical blow landed, stronger than the first. Campbell's eyes rolled up in his head, and he lost consciousness.

"I think his wards are down," I said as I followed Isabella. I hoped that Dr. Wilcox would help me cover our retreat, but he almost beat me to the door. Chivalry truly was dead among Humans.

Isabella trotted toward the boathouse, one hand wrapped around Mary's arm, the other holding her paintball gun. I heard crashing and banging from the house behind us and increased my pace.

A demon came around the corner of the house. Both Isabella and I shot it, and it veered off howling in another direction. I saw Wilcox throw a glowing ball of energy or something at a demon coming around the house from the other direction.

We fought off three more demons while getting everyone in the boat. Mary started the engine, and we pulled away from the shore. I lay Campbell on a bunk in one of the two cabins and checked to make sure he was still breathing. He was.

Looking back toward shore, I saw Campbell's home erupt in flames.

CHAPTER 17

"Where do you want me to go?" Mary asked as she steered the boat away from shore and pushed the throttle full open.

"Do you know who the healer is who treated Nieminen?" Isabella asked in answer.

The woman shrugged. "Of course. I'm the one who treated him."

I stared at her for a minute, completely caught off guard. "Why didn't you or Lord Campbell simply tell us that at the beginning?" I blurted out.

"We didn't know who was hunting him or why. He told us he was trying to protect the artifact from a cabal of blood mages."

"That seems to be the standard story," I said with a chuckle. "I've used it myself, although I'm the only one I believe."

She shot me a glance, one corner of her mouth crooked up, and I caught a twinkle in her eye.

"Is he okay?" she asked, looking toward the stairs down to the cabins.

"I think so. If you want to check on him, I can steer straight out into open water until you get back."

Without a moment's hesitation, she stood from her seat and rushed toward the stairs. I sat down and grabbed the wheel. I knew the bay was several miles wide at that point, and as long as we were headed away from the demons, I was happy.

Isabella came and sat down beside me. "Where to now?"

"I'm open to suggestions," I said. "We were looking for Nieminen and the statue, and I think we found them."

"Yeah. Be careful what you wish for," she said. "Hell, Kellana, I don't have any idea how we're going to take the statue away from him."

"You distract him, and while he's killing you, I'll sneak in and steal it."

She grimaced, then said, "I guess I deserve that."

Mary came back a few minutes later. "He's sleeping normally. I don't think the shock hurt him any, but he's not as strong as he used to be."

"Have you been with him a long time?" I asked.

"All my life." She gave me a half-smile. "I'm Mary Campbell. He's my grandfather. North or south?"

It turned out that Campbell had a slip at the Annapolis Yacht Club, so we decided to go north, figuring we would stand out less in Annapolis. I called Wen-li and asked her to meet us there. The small, picturesque city was basically split by an inlet of the bay, with a bridge connecting the two sides. I had often driven over there for a peaceful afternoon followed by a sumptuous seafood dinner.

Mary steered the boat into the harbor at Annapolis, pulled into the slip, and shut down the engine. She climbed down to the cabin to check on her grandfather while I tied the boat to the dock. I didn't feel any magic users close, but we had been attacked so many times that I was wary.

The sound of a bullet ricocheting off the side of the boat was followed by the sound of the rifle shot. Before I met Isabella, it had been decades since anyone had shot at me, but I didn't need any reminding to recognize the sound. There wasn't any kind of cover on the dock, so I dove in the water. Swimming under the boat, I came up on the other side.

The first sounds I heard when my head broke the water were more gunshots coming from multiple places. Not only single shots, but the chatter of a machinegun. Something large passed over me and splashed into the water. Treading water, I pulled out my athame and waited. I was so relieved when a jaguar poked her head above the surface a few feet away from me that I wanted to cheer.

"I think we've been betrayed," I said. Isabella swam over to me and licked my cheek with a very large tongue. That people with guns were firing at a boat in the middle of the city was pretty shocking.

In the previous two weeks, I'd done a lot of research on jaguars. Contrary to most cats, jaguars liked the water and were good swimmers, often taking alligators and caimans as prey.

"Can you float down under the bridge and come out on the other side?" I asked her.

She yawned and rubbed the top of her head against my arm. I took that as a yes.

"I'm going to swim under the boat and the docks," I said. "Work my way around the far side and come out on the other side of the yacht club. We can flank them from behind."

Another yawn, and she launched herself in the direction of the bridge. I took a deep breath and dove.

I had to come up for air three times, making sure each time that I came out under one of the docks. The first two times I surfaced, I heard gunshots, but silence greeted me the third time. By swimming under boats and docks, I was able to get around the place where I thought the shooters were stationed.

I slid out of the water and drew my sword. While I was sure the demonbane would be fatally toxic to a Human, I wasn't sure how fast it would act. Like a fool, I had left my sleepy-gas balls at home.

A man with an automatic rifle crouched behind a piling rising above one of the side docks. I crept up behind him and lay the blade of my sword on his shoulder, the length of the blade extending in front of him where he could clearly see it. He froze in place.

"If you value your head, gently set the gun down," I said. He complied. "Now, put your hands straight out to the side, as far from your body as you can." Again, he complied.

"Now, listen to me very, very carefully. I am going to ask you a few questions. The first lie or refusal to answer, and I will cut off your head. Nod if you understand." I pushed the blade into his skin enough that he started to bleed. He nodded.

"Who told you to shoot at that boat?" I asked, pushing the sword a bit deeper.

"Agent Bronski."

"And what reason did he give you? Or are you just a mercenary?"

A slight hesitation, and I pushed a little more on the blade. I hadn't cut anything vital, but blood poured out onto his white shirt.

"The mages responsible for Arlington are on board."

"I see." I drew the blade away and slammed the flat of it across the side of his head. He dropped to the ground, unconscious. Raising the sword again, I brought it down and cut the rifle in half.

I checked the man's pockets and found credentials identifying him as an FBI agent. It was too late to call off Isabella, but on the other hand I wasn't sure I wanted to. For all I knew, three of the people I had been on the boat with were dead. Of course, all three were mages. Even if Campbell was unable to respond, hopefully Wilcox or Mary could cast a defensive spell.

The next shooter I encountered went down without a whimper when the flat of my blade took him in the side of the head. I didn't have much sympathy for men who would shoot without knowing who they were shooting at.

Working my way up from the dock level to the deck where the Yacht Club members had drinks on pleasant afternoons, I peeked around the corner of the building and saw Bronski standing by the railing with his back to me.

Taking out my athame, I threw it. It stuck in Bronski's back with a solid sound, a bit softer than when I threw it at a tree. He didn't move at first. Then he slowly turned and faced me.

"Good afternoon, Miss Rogirsdottir," he said, raising a pistol toward me. His face betrayed no pain or any evidence that a knife was buried in his back.

The gun went off, and the bullet passed over me as I dove forward and to the side. Rolling and coming to my feet, I leapt high in the air toward him, and the next bullet passed under me. My feet landed on Bronski's chest, and his pistol flew through the air. He landed on his back, right on the knife, cried out, and arched in pain. But when he rolled to the side, I saw that the knife had not completely penetrated.

A bullet popped, splitting the air near my head. I looked up and saw a man with a rifle aiming at me. His gun fired again, and the bullet went wide as he pitched forward with a jaguar clinging to his back.

I was very aware that Bronski was a mage, so I

treated him to the flat of my blade. Bending over his unconscious body, I ripped his jacket apart to discover my athame stuck in some kind of stiff vest he was wearing.

"Drop your weapon and put your hands in the air," a voice over a loudspeaker boomed out.

It had taken them long enough to get there, but police cars with flashing lights sat on the bridge. Policemen with guns and vests swarmed the area. A large spotted cat bounded past me and leaped over the railing. Without a thought, I dove after her. We hit the water, and I pulled hard to get some depth.

In the shelter of one of the docks, I rose with my face barely breaking the surface and took a deep breath, then sank and swam on. I managed to avoid detection and swam underwater past the bridge and beyond until I crawled out of the water over a hundred yards upstream. The sun was sinking low in the sky. Keeping to the shadows, I crept between two houses and out to the street.

"I hate you a lot," I told Isabella when I found her sitting on the curb waiting for me. She and her clothes were dry.

Isabella looked me up and down. I felt like a used dishrag, so I could imagine what I looked like, dripping water and completely bedraggled.

"It's not something I control," she said. "I don't even know how it works. Hell, when I was young, I barely wore clothes at all. Who needs clothes in Yucatan? Besides, can't you wiggle your nose or something to take care of that?"

I cast a spell that dried me for the most part and sat down beside her. I still needed to brush my hair.

"It was Bronski," I said.

"Yeah, I saw. Why didn't you kill him?"

"I tried, but then I decided it would be better to keep him alive and try to find out why he did it."

"Should have killed him."

I sighed. "You're probably right. What do you think we should do now? Do you suppose the Campbells and Wilcox are okay?"

"They're mages. Maybe. Those guys shot up the boat pretty good."

"Why did we run?" I asked.

"Do you want to try and explain that we're the good guys and the FBI are the bad guys? The cops will turn us over to Bronski in a heartbeat."

CHAPTER 18

I donned a glamour so I would look like Isabella's sister, and we hiked over to the bus station. Soon we were on our way back to DC. We spent the time on the bus with Isabella trying to teach me Spanish.

Once back in DC, we learned the metro line between Union Station and Bethesda was closed due to demons. We took the local bus to Georgetown and then walked to my house. We discovered the house was being watched when Wen-li showed up at my door less than five minutes after we arrived.

"Should I open the door?" I asked Isabella as I peered out through a gap in the curtains. "Last time didn't work out very well."

Looking closer, I realized that it wasn't the creased-pantsuit, hair-and-makeup-perfect Wen-li that I had always seen. It wasn't even the fashion-perfect tactical warrior Wen-li that had trekked to the crater with us that night. The woman I was looking at wore jeans, a t-shirt and a clip that held her hair in a messy bun. One could even say she looked furtive, hugging what little shadow fell across my front stoop.

Since it was my summer to do dumb things, I opened the door. The cool, confident young agent I had known looked up at me with hope and fear in her face. The smell of fear was so strong I was surprised the girl was still standing. I opened the screen, reached out and grabbed her upper arm, then pulled her through the door.

Isabella retained her silent speed when she shifted to her Human form. She glided across my living room in an instant and stopped inches from Wen-li. "What happened?" she demanded.

"They—they tried to kill me. Someone. Someone tried to kill me."

"Bronski?" I asked.

Her head whipped around to stare at me. "Maybe. I think." She stopped, took a deep breath, and seemed to take hold of herself. "Yes. It would have to be."

"You told him we were going to Annapolis," I said.

"Yes. No. What I mean is I told George Foster, my boss while Dave Torbert is out of town. He told Bronski to meet you in Annapolis. I went with Foster to Campbell's house." Wen-li shook her head. "It's gone. Burned to the ground." She hunched her shoulders a bit. "We found your car. It's completely destroyed."

"Where is Torbert?" I asked.

"He's had a vacation scheduled forever. Jim, our boss, thought we could get by without him for a couple of weeks."

"Go on," I said. "Where did someone try to kill you? At Campbell's house?" I took her hand, led her into the kitchen, and pushed her into a chair. Then I put the kettle on. A little magic helped it to boil faster.

"No. When I got home. On our way back to DC, we heard that you had murdered Lord Campbell and his granddaughter, attacked our agents, and then escaped. George said we would sort it out in the morning, so I went home. When I went to open the door—the outside door to my apartment building—a man came at me and tried to shoot me."

She took another deep breath but started shaking and hyperventilating. Isabella looked alarmed and shot me a look of entreaty. I opened a cabinet and took down a bottle of dark-green liquid, poured some in a glass, and walked over to Wen-li. I didn't try to hand her the glass, just held it to her mouth and said, "Drink."

I poured a healthy swallow into her mouth, and her eyes bugged out.

"Swallow it," I commanded. She did, and her eyes started to water.

"What?" she gasped. "What was that?" She panted a little as she stared at the glass.

"*Agavirna*," I said, setting the glass on the table. I noticed that her hands had mostly stopped shaking. "It does a good job of steadying the nerves."

"And blowing the top of your head off," Wen-li said. "What proof is that stuff?"

I must have looked puzzled because Isabella asked, "What is the alcohol percentage?" She reached for the bottle, and I handed it to her. She sniffed it and her eyes widened.

"About fifty percent when it's first distilled." I shrugged. "I don't monitor it that closely. This has been aged, so it might be a little stronger due to evaporation."

"It burns like a blowtorch," Wen-li said.

"It's completely safe to drink in moderation," I replied. Deciding that after the day I'd had, a drink wasn't a bad idea, I pulled out two more glasses and poured some for Isabella and myself.

"You make this?" Isabella asked.

"Yes." I pointed to the open cabinet where three bottles with different shades of green liquid sat. "Depending on the infusion and how long it ages, you get a different drink. This is the twenty-year batch I just bottled last year."

"So," Isabella said to Wen-li, "after you killed the guy, what happened next?"

Wen-li bit her lip. "I-I went inside the building. I wanted to call George."

"Did you go inside your apartment?" Isabella prompted.

The girl shook her head. "No. There was something, something magical. Some kind of trap, I think." She took another sip of the *agavirna*. "I went back outside, out the back door. I tried to call George, but he didn't answer. I called the office, and they said George was on his way to the hospital. He and Jim Roberts, the head of PCU, had been ambushed and shot outside our headquarters."

She looked at me. "I didn't know where else to go, so I came here."

"You don't think we killed the Campbells and attacked those FBI agents?"

She shook her head, almost violently. "Bronski called me. He wanted me to meet him, but not at the office. I don't trust him."

"Good call," Isabella said. Her eyes turned up to me in an I-told-you-so look.

"Okay, I should have killed him when I had the chance," I told Isabella. I looked down at Wen-li. "You still didn't say why you came here."

She hadn't taken her eyes off me. "Dave told me you're an Elf, and he told me about Elves. He said you're an honorable person, and that as long as people acted with honor toward you, you would act with honor toward them. He said that's the way Elves are. That's very similar to the culture I was raised in. I just didn't know where else to go."

I wondered, not for the first time, how Torbert knew so much about Elves.

"We like to think of ourselves that way," I said.

"And I think most Humans like to view themselves as good people."

"How old are you?" Isabella asked in a gentle voice.

"Twenty-six. I guess you think I'm pretty young and silly."

"I don't blame you for being scared," the shifter said. "We will try to protect you, but we tried to protect the Campbells. There are no guarantees in this world."

Shortly after midnight, with everyone carrying as much in the way of food and supplies as we could, I led our small party out my back gate. We headed for Glover-Archbold Park and the clandestine trail to my nursery. If I had to defend a place, I'd rather take on mages or men with guns at the nursery instead of the townhouse.

I walked in front with Karen following me. Sometime during the evening, I had decided that Karen was easier than Special Agent Wen-li. Isabella took up the rear. As crazy as things had gotten, I was on edge. It seemed as though just going to the market had become a dangerous adventure.

I smiled but didn't slow down when I heard Isabella's snarl, followed by an Imp's squeal and then the meaty thump of the little demon hitting a rock or a tree. I doubted the creature would try her a second time.

But in spite of all the demons running around Washington, the old irritants of the park were still out in force. I came around a corner in the trail, and a Vampire jumped out in front of me. He grabbed my arms and attempted to stare into my eyes to enthrall me. He was a head shorter than I was, and when I lifted my knee between his legs, it launched him completely off the ground.

"Wrong girl, vermin," I said as I whipped my sword out of my bag. He stumbled away, and I followed, thinking about the next girl he might attack, as well as the other girls he had probably assaulted. He dodged my first cut, but I took his head on the backswing.

"Holy shit!" Karen said from behind me.

"You have to be careful out here," I said as I wiped my sword clean on his pants. "Some of the Vampires let their victims live, but not all. Check the statistics your government doesn't publish about this park. Rapes by Vampires and Werewolves are daily occurrences."

"This is one of the wealthiest areas of town," she said.

"Yeah. Think of what it's like in the parts of town the cops don't care about."

"It probably wasn't a safe place to walk at night before the breach," Isabella said.

"No, it wasn't," I answered. "I think we can thank the Vampires for taking care of the Human predators who used to come here. It's all non-Humans now. Your Darwin fellow would have loved this place."

We had one other encounter with a Vampire near to where we exited the park, but he backed off in a hurry. Then we approached the nursery.

"Stay here," I said, leaving my companions in a small grove of trees at the edge of the park. "I'm going to scout and see how many watchers we have. I want to keep everyone guessing as to where we are."

I moved away from Karen and Isabella, shrunk to

my smaller size, and donned a glamour. It took me an hour to travel the length of the fence surrounding the nursery. Two different FBI cars, two mages—as far as I could tell they weren't together—and a pair of Werewolves—who were together—had the place staked out. It bothered me that I hadn't seen more. I realized that I was viewing the situation the way a Human would. I'd been living among them for too long.

Taking off my boots, I stood with my bare feet on the ground, closed my eyes, and felt the world around me. I soon recognized the watchers I'd already identified, but also another mage, a pair of mages, and a mage waiting with five Humans. The last three groups were hidden by either spells or illusions, but the displacement of the natural world revealed them to my senses when I truly listened.

Interestingly, three of the watching people or groups were within fifteen yards of each other near the bamboo grove under the oak tree at the northwest corner of my property. The two FBI cars were just out of sight of each other near the entrance to the nursery. The Werewolves had stationed themselves on a cross street where the entrance could be seen using binoculars. But no one had staked out the northeast corner.

I went back and retrieved Isabella and Karen, and we took a long, looping route north of the nursery and then back to the northeast corner.

A low branch of the oak tree there hung over the fence thirteen feet above the ground. I leaped up, caught it, and scrambled to pull myself up on top of the branch. A quick trip to the equipment shed, and I had a sturdy rope in hand. I fashioned a loop in one end and dropped it down to where Isabella and Karen awaited.

Karen weighed practically nothing, and I pulled her up with ease. Isabella shifted and easily leaped to the top of the branch. Isabella and I slipped down the tree trunk, then I caught Karen when she jumped.

As far as I could tell, none of the outside watchers had seen us, but a large number of Fairies had roused themselves and come out to enjoy the entertainment. I spoke with their queen, and she promised to double the normal night guard.

We slipped into the cottage and I put Karen on the couch. A rug and a fluffy blanket by the door did fine for Isabella, who preferred to sleep as a cat anyway. I hoped things would shake out and return to normal soon, but I couldn't put my employees at risk. It was Thursday, and after sending out a text blast to my employees telling them not to come in to work until Monday, I fell into bed. It had been one hell of a long and disturbing day.

CHAPTER 19

My employees were always off on Sundays, so that was what it felt like at the nursery that Friday morning—very quiet, except for the Fairies, though their noise was always cheerful. With no Humans around, Fred and Kate were out tending their garden, but they were never noisy.

I was preparing breakfast when Isabella asked, "Are we just going to sit in here and wait for everyone to forget about us?"

"Do you have a better idea?" I asked, while pouring tea in her cup. "I'm not sure why everyone hasn't forgotten about us already, but I have a theory. I think Nieminen can use the jaguar statue, but he can't unlock its full potential, and he thinks you can."

She gave me a raised-eyebrow look. "And all the others?" she asked waving her arm to indicate all the watchers encircling us.

"As for the others, they aren't sure what the artifact can do, but they believe that you know. I think Nakamura has the Weres watching us. I doubt we have to worry about them—they're just watching. Vance isn't stupid enough to challenge me again. I think at least one of the FBI cars reports to Bronski, and I think the mage with the five Humans either reports to Bronski, or he is Bronski."

"I can't believe Bronski is stupid enough to want the damned thing," Karen said. "He's seen what it can do, and he certainly doesn't have the power to control it."

Setting a plate with an omelet in front of her, I said, "Bronski doesn't strike me as smart enough or ambitious enough to go after the statue on his own. I think he's working for someone else—a more powerful mage."

"What about the other FBI car?" Karen asked.

"Either they're all together, or maybe one group is actually on the side of the law."

"Or two different FBI factions are trying to snatch the statue," Isabella said.

Karen's cell phone rang and she pulled it out. "It's Dave!" She answered, "Where are you? Things are a complete disaster here."

She talked to him for about twenty minutes, filling him in on the latest events. I knew Isabella had excellent hearing, but I didn't know if she could hear Torbert's side of the conversation as well as I could. So, when Karen hung up, I let her tell us of their conversation.

"Agent Torbert said he's coming back to DC, but it's going to take a couple of days," Karen announced. "Some of our superiors at the Bureau contacted him. He told me to stay here, to stay with you."

"And Bronski?" I asked. I had heard her tell Torbert of her suspicions about Bronski.

"Dave said he will issue orders to have him detained. He also gave me the name and number of someone in DC to contact. He said the man is a mage and he can help to relieve the pressure on us."

I had heard that. Miika Apthenir seemed to be a personal friend of Torbert's and not someone connected to the PCU or the FBI.

After breakfast, Karen called Torbert's friend. She spoke with him briefly, then he broke the connection.

"He refuses to speak over the phone," Karen said. "He said that if we want his help, Kellana ap th'Rogir needs to meet him at the National Gallery of Art this afternoon. Is that your name?"

I found myself nodding my head. "It's one form of my name."

Isabella argued that it was too dangerous. Then she wanted to go with me. Karen tried to call Torbert back, but he didn't answer. Finally, I agreed to go and meet with Miika ap th'Tenir, as I suspected his name was properly pronounced. Karen called him back, but he didn't answer either.

I knew where NGA was, the problem was getting there. I had a mental vision of driving out of the nursery and leading a parade to downtown. Instead, I had to climb the oak tree, drop down on the other side of the fence, shrink to my smaller size, then walk two blocks to ensure I was beyond watching eyes. Two blocks when your legs are more than three feet long is no big deal. Two blocks when your legs are six inches long turned out to be quite a hike.

Then I had to wait for a bus, which was late. It took me almost two hours from the time I left the nursery until I got to the National Mall. I hoped the mystery man I was supposed to meet would wait for me.

The east wing of the gallery was the modern art section, a separate building with a street between it and the main museum. I tended to avoid places where they wanted to check my bag, such as museums, concert halls, and government buildings. I donned a glamour that hid the bag, and entered the museum's west wing, then went downstairs to the gift shop and through the tunnel to the east wing.

Miika had an advantage over me. I had no idea what he looked like. Karen had told him I was tall with green hair. Of course, if he wasn't wearing a glamour, he should be easy to spot. The moving walkway in the tunnel spit me out into the basement gift shop. Other than a few tourists and their kids, I didn't see anyone unusual or feel any magic.

The top three floors surrounded an empty space in the center. A wide, open stairway along one wall led from the basement to the first floor, then to the second, then up to the third. I would be visible to anyone in the museum the entire way. Standing at the base of the stairway, I scanned what I could see, trying to feel any magic in the building.

Silver-blonde hair past his shoulders, silver eyes, and a face far too beautiful for a Human caught my eye. He leaned on the edge of the railing on the third floor. Then he saw me. His gaze locked onto me and didn't waver as I climbed the three flights to his level. Halfway up the last flight of stairs, I began to feel his magic, a magic unlike any I had felt in Earth's realm. A magic I hadn't felt since Midgard.

He was short and stout for a male Elf, at most an inch taller than I was, with a broad chest and shoulders. The lines of his face were muted. Although too beautiful for Hollywood, he wasn't beautiful enough for the palace in Elhandirhin in Alfheim. But his kind were relatively common in Midgard, where I spent my first one hundred and twenty years.

"Sel Kellana," he said in greeting, properly dipping his head and awarding me a half-bow. A certain lilt in his voice was common in Midgard but not in Alfheim. That made sense. Humans were rare in Alfheim.

"Serin Miika," I answered. I felt awkward. I was just a farm girl, not of noble birth. The artificial divisions and unfathomable prejudices Humans imposed on each other in Earth's realm suddenly made the class and race divisions of Midgard seem petty and meaningless. He addressed me as 'Sel' and I addressed him as 'Serin' rather than 'Ser' automatically. It was drilled into both of us from birth. His father may have been royalty for all I knew, but I was deemed superior to him because my mother was an Elf and his was Human.

"Ser Miika," I corrected, elevating him to my equal. His was a face from home, and how much that meant to me was almost overwhelming.

He jerked, almost as though I had slapped him, then leaned forward, studying my face.

"We are far from Midgard," I said in Elvish, "and we have far more commonalities than differences in this realm. I come to you for help, and I ask, Ser, for I have no right or ability to command."

He didn't answer, but he also didn't turn on his heel and leave. I think he was trying to decide if I was mocking him.

"David Torbert said that you might be able to help us. I don't know how much he told you of the situation."

"He really didn't tell me anything except that one of his people, Karen Wen-li, was in danger and that she was currently under the protection of an Elf who called herself Kellana Rogirsdottir. He told me the PCU is under assault and asked if I could help." A brief smile crossed his face. "I do some paid consulting work for the PCU from time to time."

"I am not a mage," I said, "Only a witch and alchemist. Karen is a Human witch. We are faced by mages and demons and a great evil, our only aid that of a cat shifter."

Closing my eyes for a moment, I truly felt the magic of the man standing in front of me.

I opened my eyes and blurted, "You're a battle mage?"

That brief smile again. "My father was. I have had some training, but my magic is that of a halfling, not an Elf."

But strong. Perhaps stronger than James Campbell, who was the strongest Human mage I had encountered other than Aleksi Nieminen. And halflings were known to have some unique magic. Alfheim had used them as shock troops for millennia. Miika probably wasn't any stronger physically than I was, and he definitely wouldn't be as fast or heal as well as I did. One thing I had not seen from any of the mages involved in hunting the statue was battle magic, or at least nothing in the class of Elven battle magic.

"Do you drink coffee?" he asked.

"Yes, I do."

He switched to English. "Let's go get a cup and you can brief me."

An hour later, after listening to my tale, he leaned back in his seat and smiled. A true, happy-looking smile.

"I do believe I can help. I have what I think might be a valuable attribute. I'm a realm walker."

"Danu merde," I breathed. I was looking at a man who could take me home.

I tried to pay the bill, but he took it from me. He held the door for me, both entering and exiting the café. He held my door when we reached his car, a dark green BMW that probably cost four times the price of my poor destroyed Honda.

We drove up to Chevy Chase, and when he turned into a residential neighborhood, I grinned as we passed several of my wealthy clients' homes. He turned into the driveway of a mansion that didn't need my services and I felt us slide through the wards surrounding the place. Someone had done a wonderful, if somewhat eclectic, job with the landscaping.

He parked the car in a five-car garage, the other bays also holding luxury cars. We entered the house through a side door, and he led me through the kitchen and dining room to a large sitting room.

"Make yourself comfortable while I put some equipment together," he said.

While he was doing that, he asked me a number of questions. Instead of trying to give him piecemeal answers, I told him the story of meeting Isabella, the event in Arlington, the sacrifice of Jennifer Watkins, and the attack on James Campbell and the PCU.

"I don't know where Aleksi Nieminen is, or how to stop him," I concluded. "I do know that I can't hunt him while I'm pinned down in my compound. I don't even know who all my enemies are, or how many sides there are in all of this."

Out of the blue, Miika asked, "Do you cook?"

I was taken aback and didn't know what to say. I tried to put a smile on my face. "People say I'm a pretty good cook, although I can't get all the ingredients I'd use in Midgard."

"I'm in," he said, and winked at me. "You can't imagine how much I've missed home cooking."

CHAPTER 20

I knocked on the window of the Werewolves' Mercedes. The man closest to me looked over, and I saw his eyes about bug out of his head.

"I thought you puppies learned your lesson," I shouted. "Tell Vance I'm not happy about this."

The driver started the engine, revved it, and took off. Or tried to. It wasn't a very impressive getaway after I had knifed all four tires. The noisy flapping of the tire rubber sort of ruined the drama.

We didn't know what the men in the FBI cars were doing, or whose side they were on, so I dealt with both cars the same way. When they rolled down their windows, I shot their cars full of sleepy gas.

Two mages sat on either side of the bamboo grove where they could watch the cottage. The fairies had watched them since they first arrived and reported there was no evidence the mages knew about each other. I crept close enough to get a feel for each mage's magic and reported back to Miika.

We discussed what I reported and devised a plan. When the Fairies suddenly boiled out of the bamboo grove hurling spears, the two unknown mages failed to protect their rears. I stepped up behind one mage and hit him over the head with a hammer. Miika stepped up behind the other one, laid his hands on the guy, and sucked his magic and consciousness from him. From that point, it was a simple matter for the Fairies to grab the mages by their clothing, carry them inside the grove, and for me to set a ward around it.

"That was a pretty neat trick," I told Miika. "I don't suppose a witch can learn it?"

He shook his head. "No, but I know a rune spell that is similar."

I tried to tone down my smile, afraid I might blind him.

Miika dealt with another of the mages by simply walking up to him and asking if he was ready to die. The man, who turned out to be one of those who bid on the statue when Weber had it, took Miika's measure and decided to go back to Los Angeles. A band of Fairies followed him to his car and watched him drive away.

That left the two groups that worried me the most. The Fairies confirmed that Bronski, who they knew because he had been to the compound before, was there with five other Humans, set up in a picnic shelter in the public park. The Fairies also reported the Humans were armed with 'weird-shaped clubs', and the pictures they drew in the air showed the shape of assault rifles.

Considering Bronski's willingness to use guns in Annapolis, I worried about my friends as well as the Fairies and Pixies in the area. What would happen if a bullet didn't hit anything? Would it keep going until it did? I didn't know.

Then there was the pair of mages who had taken up station by the oak at the front of my property. I didn't recognize them, but their magic felt strong and dark.

And these people were only the side show. We had no idea where Nieminen was or what he was doing. A nagging voice in the back of my mind said that he was planning something. He had seen what he could do in Arlington. Suppose he decided to do that someplace like New York or London? What was his ultimate objective? Isabella and I had discussed that, and neither of us liked any of the answers we could imagine.

Isabella volunteered to come out of the compound to help us, but I wanted someone besides Karen inside. In spite of the impressive abilities of my new ally, I trusted the jaguar shifter more than anyone on the planet. I knew she could take care of business.

"I think we should deal with the warriors first," Miika said. "The mage they have is far weaker than those others."

"Can you protect yourself against bullets?" I asked. "I can set stationary wards, but I've never tried to shield myself from bullets."

"How is your archery?" he asked.

I pulled out my bow, as did he. I called a Fairy to me, and three flew over. I asked them if the men were wearing vests. It took a little bit of back and forth questions and interpretation, but they finally confirmed that the Humans were wearing vests.

"Miika, in Annapolis, Bronski and his men wore bullet-proof vests. That means you can't shoot them in the body."

The Fairies helped us to find trees that had a clear view of Bronski's forces, and Miika and I climbed into separate ones. Mindful of the Humans' guns, we decided that each archer would take no more than two shots from a given stand. If we were spotted, we would get the hell out.

"A whole lot easier to come back and try again when you're alive," Miika said, and I fervently agreed.

Two of Bronski's men were outside the picnic shelter, stationed apart from each other and watching the compound through binoculars.

I was trying to figure out the best shot to take on a

crouching Human wearing body armor when the man I was watching sprouted an arrow from the side of his head. The suddenness of it startled me. I shifted my eyes to the man farther away and saw him jerk, then fall over with an arrow sticking out of his eye.

Miika's statement that he had "some training" in the battle arts was obviously Elven distraction. I considered myself an excellent archer, but that last shot was over a hundred yards. The halfling crawled down his tree on the side away from the picnic shelter and snuck away, following a Fairy to his next tree stand.

We waited. Almost two hours later, two men emerged and walked to where the dead men lay.

The man closest to me reached his comrade, and when he saw the man was dead, stopped and looked up. My arrow took him in the throat, and he went down without a sound. I looked around for the farther man but didn't see him. After scanning the area more slowly, I saw him lying face down on the ground with an arrow sticking out of his neck.

Shortly thereafter, another man came out of the shelter. He called out a name, evidently wondering where all his comrades had gone. My arrow hit his throat, while Miika's entered his eye. I slid to the ground on the side of the tree away from the shelter and crawled over to another large tree. I climbed it, nocked another arrow and waited.

We waited for half an hour, then a black ball sailed out of the shelter, hit the ground, and rolled. A thin stream of black smoke rose from it. I had a bad feeling and immediately slid out of the tree on the side away from the shelter and started running. Behind me, starting rather softly, I heard an ear-splitting siren sound that grew louder and louder. Glancing back over my shoulder, I saw an ugly black cloud billowing toward me.

The sonics of the spell were disorienting, and I tried to shut it out, concentrating on reaching my compound. A Fairy spun in the air, hands over her ears and a look of anguish on her face. I snatched her out of the air as I passed.

I reached the fence around my compound before the smoke reached me. I vaulted the fence, hitting on my feet and rolling on the other side. Beyond it, the park I had just vacated was filled with the smoke. Fairies and Pixies streamed over the fence toward me. The Pixies almost never came inside. The park was theirs, and my compound belonged to the Fairies. Two wars between them had established that decades before.

A few Pixies and a couple of Fairies were caught by the smoke. They dropped from the air, hit the ground, and didn't move. The smoke stopped at my wards, a roiling, oily, stinking cloud. Birds dropped from the trees, and I could see flowers and bushes wilting.

I stared at it in horror. The evil required to even think of such a spell was beyond my understanding. Miika had not made it inside my wards. I prayed to the Goddess that he either managed to escape in another direction or ward himself.

Isabella and Karen came running from the cottage, stopping when they reached me. The horrified expressions on their faces mirrored what I was feeling.

Then Isabella changed. She crouched and gathered herself, then launched herself up toward the fence.

"No!" I reached out and grabbed a handful of her

hide. She was so powerful that she lifted me off the ground, but I was strong enough to pull her back. Rounding on me, she snarled, but I didn't let go.

"Don't be stupid," I said. "Look. It killed Pixies and Fairies. Magical beings. I know you're strong, but you don't even know what kind of spell it is."

She snarled at me again.

"No. You can't," I said. "I can't lose you. I need you."

Again, she snarled, and snapped at my hand, but I didn't let go. Then I felt the tension drain from her body, and abruptly she shifted back to her Human form.

"Sweet mother. What kind of monster would do such a thing?"

"Evil," Karen said. "There is evil in the world, and there's your proof. That's why I joined the Bureau."

"I hope there weren't any people, any children, out there." I looked around. The Pixie village had over a hundred inhabitants, maybe two hundred. Children and babies.

The Fairy queen lit on my shoulder. She told me that the Pixies had taken their young underground when the bad Humans first arrived. But some had obviously been caught out by the spell, and a couple of dozen Fairies were unaccounted for.

A few minutes later we heard the first sirens. The park was bordered by residential neighborhoods on three sides, and people would have reported the viscous black cloud.

A police car pulled up in front of my gate, and I went out to talk to them.

"Are you all right, miss?" an older cop asked me.

"Yes, but I have no idea what that is. It feels evil,"

I told him.

He craned his neck, looking inside my compound. The black cloud pushed right up against the fence on the park side but came no further. He eyed me with suspicion.

"I had wards set by a witch," I told him. "It's cheaper than hiring a night watchman. I guess I got my money's worth, but I have nothing to do with that...whatever it is."

That got me looks that said I was crazy, but I didn't care. Better crazy than criminal.

Soon there were lots of cops, FBI, military, ambulances, and helicopters—some official and some from the news media. In the midst of it all, Miika strolled in through the front gate. He had Fairies and Pixies clinging onto his hair and clothing and peeking out of his pockets. The Fairies were pretty freaked out, but the Pixies looked as though they were in shock.

"Thank the Goddess you're safe," I said, pulling him into the compound, away from all the insanity outside and toward the cottage. Once inside, I poured him a shot of *agavirna*. He downed it in a single swallow.

"Very nice," he said. "I approve." Then he fell into a chair and leaned over with his elbows on his knees and his hands covering his face. "That was bad," he said.

The Fairies rarely came into the cottage, but they were flying all over the place, and so were the Pixies, fussing over those Miika brought with him.

"I saved as many as I could," he said, straightening up, and I could see tears in his eyes. "I couldn't save them all. I can't believe that unholy bastard was willing to poison the earth to strike back at us."

"No honor," I said. "How did you get out?"

"I cast a shielding spell. The cloud is starting to dissipate now, but the wind carried it into the houses north of the park. I think they're running out of ambulances. I've seen battle in numerous realms, but never anything like that."

Television reporters came to the gate several times, wanting to talk with us because we were so close to the cloud. Some tried to ask about why it didn't come past my fence. I refused to speak with any of them.

Isabella reported that the two dark mages who were hanging around earlier had left.

"Too many witnesses," Miika said.

"Afraid of being blamed for that spell if anyone suspected they were mages," Karen countered.

CHAPTER 21

By the following morning, Miika and two mages contracted to the PCU declared the park safe to enter. Humans still wore hazmat suits to enter the park, and I wore rubber hip waders and surgical gloves. The beautiful park was a wasteland. I hadn't seen anything that bleak and foreboding since 1945. Rhoslyn, the Fairy queen, reported that a dozen Fairies and between thirty and forty Pixies had been caught by the spell.

I approached a woman in a hazmat suit who appeared to be in charge of documenting the damage. She told me they had counted more than three hundred dead birds and dozens of dead squirrels. She and her team had also noted the Fairies and Pixies, who were in the process of recovering their dead. In addition, more than a dozen Humans living in the area around the park had died.

"As far as I can tell, not a blade of grass survived," she said. "Trees, bushes, flowers, all turned that ash color. The only things that are still alive are the branches of those two oak trees that hang over the park from your property, and that bamboo grove over there. Do you mind telling me why that cloud didn't penetrate your fence?"

I suddenly remembered the mages we had imprisoned. Although I wanted to find Miika and check on the mages, I realized the woman was waiting for an answer.

"Witches' wards," I told her. "I have the whole property protected."

She didn't act surprised, though it was hard to see her face through the mask she wore.

"You wouldn't happen to be the witch, would you?"

I debated several ways of dodging her question, but finally said, "Yes."

The woman nodded. "Helluva strong spell. Lucky you had it in place."

I tracked Miika down at the northern edge of the park. He stood staring at the houses across the street. Their walls were stained gray and black, and some of the materials looked as though they had melted or had acid splashed on them. A few had open windows.

"That is where the Humans died?" I asked.

"See the open windows? Where the spell found its way in, it killed everything it touched."

"What did you find in that picnic shelter?" I asked, switching to Elvish.

He shook his head. "Nothing. The police and FBI are being very tight-lipped, but I do know that they found the assault rifles of the men we killed."

"And the arrows?"

"Yes, they found those, too. The press hasn't been told about either one. In fact, other than authorized officials, you and I are the only ones they've allowed into the park."

I looked around at all the people in hazmat suits, the police cordon around the park, and all the official vehicles parked around the area. "They think we know something," I said. "Don't trust any of the PCU people. Karen doesn't want any of them to know where she is."

I leaned close to him. "The bamboo grove wasn't harmed. I think we should check on the mages we left in there."

His startled look proved that he had forgotten

about the mages, too. We walked around through the nursery gate and back to the area where the bamboo grew against the fence. Lying on the grass where we had left them were the mages Miika had spelled. I leaned down and was relieved to see that both were still breathing.

"So, what do we do with them?" I asked him.

"I don't know. What do you want to do with them?" he answered.

Isabella wandered up and scrutinized them for a couple of minutes. "Wake them up, and let them go," she said. "Make them walk out through the park and tell them that's what the statue's magic does."

Miika and I exchanged looks.

"I can't do that," I said. "That spell didn't involve the statue."

"It was a blood-magic spell, wasn't it?" she asked.

"Well, yeah."

"Then tell them that the spell was blood magic, and the jaguar statue is a blood-magic artifact. If they still want the statue, then they're too stupid to live and we'll deal with them accordingly."

Miika gave me a questioning look and I said, "Works for me."

He chanted a short spell, sketched a rune, then said a Word. The two mages stirred, and then sat up. They stared at us through the fence, looked around at their bamboo prison, then back at us.

As close as I was to them, I was able to read their magic. There was both a qualitative and quantitative difference between witches and mages. Those guys had mage magic, but they weren't much stronger than I was.

"You're looking for a jaguar statue," I said. "We

don't have it, and don't know where it is. It's a blood-magic tool, and you shouldn't want it either. Now, if you fight your way through the bamboo in that direction," I pointed, "you'll get a chance to see some blood magic first hand. If you decide that you like that sort of thing, and come back here seeking the statue again, you'll leave next time wearing a funeral shroud."

We watched them go, fighting their way through the thick bamboo along the fence line. Beyond the grove, we saw them emerge into what was left of the park. The expressions on their faces as they viewed the devastation were priceless.

One of them turned back to us and asked, "What in the hell happened?"

"An attack by a blood mage," I answered. Pointing to the bamboo, I said, "I set a ward around you to keep you out of our hair. I really didn't intend it to keep you safe, it just worked out that way. I think you can see what happened to everything outside that ward."

The other mage was watching all the emergency personnel and vehicles. A helicopter flew low overhead. He shook his head. "Did anyone die?" he asked in a shaky voice.

"Yes. Thirteen Humans, I think," Miika said. "That was the last count I heard. Plus, a number of the Fae, the little people. Birds, squirrels, all the insects."

We watched them make their way out of the park. Two cops stopped them when they got to the sidewalk. A couple more cops were called. The last I saw of the mages was when they got into an FBI car.

Torbert showed up around midnight. Isabella

came into my bedroom and woke Karen and me up so that I could let him through the wards.

No one had ever stayed at the cottage with me before I met Isabella. With four of us there, it was very tight. Karen was such a tiny thing that she shared my bed while Miika slept on the couch and Isabella on the rug by the front door. It would have been far more comfortable at my place in Georgetown.

"What in the hell has been going on here?" Torbert asked as I sat him at the kitchen table, started a pot of coffee brewing, and put some food in the oven.

Karen filled him in on the PCU end of things, then Miika told him about Bronski's attack in the park. By the time they were done, the coffee was ready, as was a loaf of fresh, hot, fruit bread.

"I can't believe they would kill Lord Campbell," Torbert said. "He's the ICAA ambassador to the U.S. government."

"And Nieminen is head of the ICAA," Isabella countered, "or at least he used to be. The chaos the statue has engendered is exactly why I was afraid of it."

"But, how did Bronski take control of the PCU?" Torbert asked.

"With you gone, Jim and George in the hospital, he just stepped in and took charge," Karen said. "He has a large number of agents who think he knows what he's doing—staving off a takeover by the alien-Godless non-Humans. After all, we're the Paranormal Crimes Unit, and there are obviously a lot of paranormal crimes being committed. I spoke with a friend there last night..." she trailed off, then said, "I guess it's still last night, isn't it? Anyway, Bronski managed to convince upper management at the

Bureau that the unit is under assault and that he's working to prevent another Arlington. Then this thing in the park happened, and everyone's running scared."

"Well, I'm back now, so he's not in charge anymore," Torbert said.

"And if he knows you're back, you'll be in the hospital or the morgue," Miika said.

"It's sheer luck that Jim and George survived," Karen said. "If they had taken me out, you would still be on vacation and wouldn't even know about all this."

"But why?" Torbert asked. "Why is Bronski doing all of this?

Isabella spoke up. "Kellana and I have discussed this, and we think it's all for distraction. The PCU was hunting Nieminen. The ICAA was hunting him. Kellana and I found him once and were on his trail again. We think Bronski is working for Nieminen. He's disrupted the PCU and taken Lord Campbell out of the equation. He's tried to kill us twice. The big question is, where is Aleksi Nieminen and what is he planning?"

CHAPTER 22

Once the sun rose, Torbert got on the phone and started calling the top people at the FBI. After an hour, he came into the kitchen and flopped down in a chair.

"This is unbelievable. Damn near everyone who can make a decision is either sick, otherwise indisposed, or just plain missing."

"What about at the Department of Justice?" Karen asked. DOJ was the FBI's parent organization.

"I can't get hold of anyone who knows anything. They keep referring me back to the Bureau."

"Don't you have friends and colleagues who will listen to you rather than Bronski?" I asked.

"Well, yeah, probably."

"Then I suggest that you forget about the bureaucracy, which as far as I can tell is barely functional at the best of times, and take charge." I put a cup of coffee on the table in front of him. "The major thing we need to do is find Aleksi Nieminen. Bronski is a minor problem."

Torbert looked out the window and gestured at the devastated park. "You consider that a minor problem?"

"Okay, find Bronski," Miika said. "If I can get within five hundred yards of him, I'll solve that problem."

The PCU agent shook his head. "I can't sanction murder. He needs to be arrested and tried for his crimes."

"Agent Torbert," I said, "have you ever been in a war before? I guarantee you're in one now. People like

Bronski and Nieminen count on people like you having scruples. Take a lesson from Agent Wen-li and don't hesitate when someone is trying to kill you."

"When were you in a war?" Torbert asked, his tone disdainful.

"The last time? Germany, nineteen forty-five. The Germans, Americans, British, and Russians all tried to kill me." I pointed at the park. "Believe me, that's what war looks like."

I was so angry I wanted to slap him. Instead, I set my coffee cup down and walked out the door. When they carried the bodies of the men Miika and I killed out of the park, it had triggered some really bad old memories. The blackened trees and blasted bushes brought back strong images of a park in Dresden after the allied firebombs. There was a time that I thought I would never escape the smell of burning flesh.

Fred's head popped up from behind a row of irises, so I wandered over to talk to him. Among the little folk that lived in the area, he paid little attention to territorial boundaries, and the fence meant nothing to him and Kate since they traveled underground into the park whenever they wanted.

He was freaked out about what had happened, and told me that in spite of heavy losses, most of the Pixies were okay. The problem was that in early summer they had little in the way of stored food. They couldn't stay where they were, but they didn't have any place to go. Most of the DC area had seen constant battles for territory after the veils fell. The band of Pixies in the park had staked their claim and successfully defended it. Now their home was a wasteland, their food supply destroyed.

Of course, Humans gave no thought to beings they rarely saw and most probably didn't believe in. I couldn't simply invite them into the nursery. Pixies and Fairies were natural rivals, and Queen Rhoslyn would never agree to share her territory.

I asked Fred to tell the Pixies to get ready to move, and I would find a place for them. Unfortunately, I thought as I watched him sink into the ground, I had no idea where that would be.

I walked among the flowers and trees, running the past few days through my mind. Isabella and I had tried to figure out what was going on. We thought the attention from both Bronski and the others interested in the statue was fostered by Nieminen, who was trying to interrupt our hunt for him. But why? He had plenty of opportunity to move out of the area, but he obviously hadn't. Why not?

But Bronski was doing more than simply trying to kill us. He was sowing chaos throughout the DC area and especially targeting its only law enforcement organization that focused solely on magic users and non-Humans.

My thoughts bounced around in a dozen different directions. I wondered if the White House grounds had Pixies or Fairies. I knew the National Arboretum had the largest tribe of Fairies in the city, but I'd never been to the White house. I'd probably need to truck the Pixies out of the city and try to find a place none of the Fae had yet settled.

After a while, my anger at Torbert bled away, and I wandered back to the cottage. I met Isabella coming out of the door.

"We need to rescue the Pixies," I said.

She stared at me as though I'd spoken in Elvish. "Okay," she said slowly. "What do you need me to do?"

I enlisted Miika to help me unload everything out

of a van, and asked Isabella to use her computer skills to find organic fruit and vegetable farms within a hundred miles of DC. By the time the van was emptied, Isabella had a list of about a dozen places.

By calling each one and asking about their farming practices, and especially about their pest control programs, I was able to determine three possible candidates. Since Pixies eat insects as well as vegetative food, and are also excellent pollinators, it was easy to figure out which farms had either Pixies or Fairies. I chose a large operation in southern Pennsylvania whose owner confessed that he was having difficulties with his insect control.

Miika cast a spell that created a tunnel of clean air from the nursery to the Pixie's underground village. We watched them fly over their scorched home, carrying their babies and everything they owned, and into the back of the van. Half an hour later, Miika and I were on the road, heading north.

We drove through Baltimore and out into the beautiful country north of there. I had to lay some ground rules for the Pixies. No more than a dozen at a time up front in the driver's section, and no crawling or sitting on the driver. None of them had ever ridden in a vehicle before, and it was a new experience. Half a dozen Pixies sat on the dashboard, and more hung from Miika's hair or sat on his shoulders. A constant reshuffling had Pixies trading places from the back of the van to the front. If they had anything in the way of material goods, I probably could have sold tickets.

When we reached the farm, I drove past and down a side road bordering the property. I stopped and we rolled down our windows. The band's chief and a couple of dozen other Pixies flew out and scouted the area. Over a period of an hour, they gradually returned, excited and happy. The chief told me that I was the most wonderful Elf who had ever lived, and I opened the back doors of the van.

Ten minutes later, Miika and I were on the road back to DC. It was a rather bittersweet moment, as I doubted I would ever see any of them again. The average lifespan of a Pixie was about five years, barring accident or predation. Winters were hard on the older ones, and the Pennsylvania climate was harsher than that of DC.

"The President has declared a state of emergency," Isabella said when we pulled into the nursery that evening.

"What does that mean?" I asked, having no idea what she was talking about.

"Come see." She wheeled about and led me into the sitting room where her laptop sat on the coffee table. Turning the screen toward me, she pointed at it. I sat down and read it, but the only thing I really understood was that some lawyer in the government had appointed Alan Bronski as head of the PCU.

Torbert was in the kitchen talking to someone on the phone. Karen hovered near him, pacing and obviously distraught.

I turned to Miika, who had been reading over my shoulder. "Do you understand what's going on?"

"The U.S. government has essentially declared war on non-Humans. All of us. Their President has called all their senators and congressmen to meet with him Thursday night. Something about a plot to take over the government." He shook his head. "You've lived here longer than I have. Don't you know how this government of theirs works?"

"No. I pay as little attention to it all as I can."

We both looked to Isabella, whose face was very grim.

"It looks as though they plan to declare martial law. That means the military taking control and rounding up all the non-Humans they can find. They'll lock us up."

"Good luck with that," Miika said. He was a realm walker, and I knew of no spell that could hold him, as long as he was breathing and conscious.

"Where is this meeting?" I asked.

"At the Capitol," Isabella said, and I saw her face clear as she worked things through in her mind. "The whole government—all the people in charge of everything—will all be in one place."

It hit me then. "Nieminen. The statue. He can take the entire government out at once. That is why he's staying in this area."

She nodded. "What I don't understand is what the end game is. What does he do after that? How does it benefit him?"

"And how does this war on non-Humans fit in?" I asked.

"Nieminen hates non-Humans," Miika said. "He has always chafed at what he considers prejudice against magic users. He thinks mages are superior beings and should rule over the non-gifted. But when the veils fell and all the non-Humans, especially beings such as Elves, the Aesir, and Angels, came through, he felt threatened. He is the major reason the ICAA admits only Human mages. An Elven or Aesirian mage would laugh at the idea of a Human mage being superior. Aleksi will use Humans' fears of demons and shifters to try and exterminate all of us."

"How do you know that?" I asked.

"He's my cousin. My mother is his grandfather's sister. I met him the first time I came to this realm, and it didn't go well. He called me an abomination." Miika barked a short laugh. "He thought I should be ashamed of my heritage, but it was the opposite side of my lineage than the Elves of Midgard thought I should be ashamed of. I've run into him a couple of times since then." He captured my eyes with his own. "You shocked me."

"I could tell. I almost fell back into the mindset of Midgard, but I'm not the woman who left there."

"No, you're not," he said, reaching out and taking my hand. He squeezed it and then let go.

"So, what do we do?" Isabella said. "We have to stop him."

"First, we have to find him," I said. "We have a clue, though. My bet is that he'll be within eighteen hundred and twenty-four yards of the Capitol."

CHAPTER 23

Torbert made the statement, "I wish to hell I knew exactly what information the President has. I'd like to know what he's thinking."

I couldn't help with the last part, but, "Suppose someone could get into the White House. How would someone find what you want?" I asked. "I mean, you want to know what Bronski and that dimwitted lawyer guy are telling him, right?"

"I think the Attorney General is acting under compulsion," Miika said.

"Whatever," I brushed him off, still looking at Torbert, who explained what he thought was a fantasy. It helped that he had been in the White House several times.

The nursery was under observation from both the police and the FBI, so we couldn't drive without being followed. Miika, Torbert, and I went over the fence early Monday morning via one of the oak trees. Torbert didn't seem to have any tree-climbing skill, so Miika carried him up and dropped him to me on the other side. He weighed less than Isabella in spite of being six inches taller than she was.

Humans' security systems had not caught up with the capabilities of non-Humans. That may have been in part because they refused to acknowledge intelligence in anything that didn't look exactly like a Human. Even with Werewolves and Werecats, Humans tended to think of them as only semi-intelligent, even when the Weres wore their Human forms.

Although Miika was a mage, he wasn't an Elf and didn't have an inherent ability to change size. He,

Dave Torbert, and I walked along Pennsylvania Avenue until we crossed Fifteenth Street. Dave and Miika turned right due to the security barricades. I shrunk, donned a glamour, and walked right by the security guards.

Once I was inside the fence, I ran the rest of the way to the building. Torbert told me that infrared sensors were the only mechanical or electronic intruder detection system. Masking my body heat was easy. Otherwise, I simply had to escape notice by the guards and other people on the property and get through doors that had badge and keypad entries. That meant I just had to find people going in or out.

I had been in a few palaces and castles in Europe as a tourist, and the White House was comparably impressive inside, made all the more so since I was seeing it while less than one-sixth of my normal height.

Torbert had gone to the Internet and printed the President's schedule for the day. It showed who he met with, when, and where. It shocked me that it was that easy. Since I also had a map of the building, arriving on time at the Oval Office for his meeting with Attorney General Adair and Alan Bronski wasn't a problem. I stood by the office door next to two guards dressed in suits and waited for the door to open.

In person, it was easy to confirm Miika's suspicions. The Attorney General was not operating under his own free will. A dozen people attended the meeting, half wearing military uniforms. Perhaps a stronger mage could have compelled them all, but Bronski didn't even try. He really didn't have to, since his puppet the Attorney General played his role perfectly.

A document explaining the crisis was handed out to each participant. Explaining that and answering questions took an hour. To say it was complete bullshit would be an understatement. Bronski blamed me for the spell that destroyed the park, and listening to him, I was almost ready to declare myself a menace to all life on Earth. Isabella was right. I should have killed him when I had the chance.

The second document was the plan for arresting all non-Humans and putting them in some sort of camps out in the wilderness all over the country. It didn't sound possible to me, but Bronski assured everyone that with the help of loyal Human mages and the support of the ICAA, he could control all the terrible monsters and send them back where they came from. He never directly came out and said he planned to exterminate us, but I could tell that several people in the room took that for granted.

The security plan for the President's Congressional speech was included with the document. There were twelve people in the room, but Bronski had brought fifteen copies, so I just had to make it out with one.

Although invisible due to my glamour, I stood well out of the way, in a fold of a curtain where I could see everyone in the room. Only a few of the men there—they were all men—seemed at all skeptical, and only two of those were in the military. Several openly displayed anger at the charges in the background document, and the smell of fear in the room was almost overwhelming.

People who were afraid were easy to manipulate, and while Bronski might have lacked in magical power, he displayed a keen ability to persuade. Of course, not being constrained by facts certainly helped. He told more lies in two hours than I could have possibly imagined. What little trust I had in Humans almost totally evaporated.

When the meeting was over, everyone left except the President and one other man. The President wrung his hands and moaned about the terrible situation. The other man didn't look convinced. Finally, the other man left. The President waited a couple of minutes, then followed him. I leaped onto his desk, grabbed a copy of each of the documents, and slipped out the door beside him.

We walked around a couple of corners with his escort following behind us. It made me sort of nervous, thinking that surely someone would detect me, but no one did. Humans hadn't yet overcome their distrust of mages enough to use them as guardians or to set wards. The weird thing was that Bronski had sold them on that exact thing. The mages—Human mages—will protect you from the non-Human monsters.

I realized the President was going to wherever he lived. The schedule I memorized showed a break for lunch after the meeting. I needed to find a way out. I was afraid that if I stopped to get my bearings, someone might step on me. We passed an open door with a sign saying "Press Briefing Room", and I ducked inside. The room was empty and memory told me the door at the other end of the room led to another room with an outside door.

To my consternation, the next room had a lot of small cubicles with small offices along the walls. And people. Lots of people. Working on laptops, talking into phones, rushing back and forth.

Sticking close to the wall, I worked my way around the room until I got to the door. That's when I ran into a minor problem. Being twelve inches tall had its drawbacks. I wasn't tall enough to reach the latch, and even if it was unlocked, I wasn't sure I was strong enough to open it. Growing back to full size would increase my chances of getting caught. I knew everyone there was engrossed in their own business, but someone would notice a person appearing from thin air.

I waited for half an hour before someone opened the door, and I slid out before the door closed. There were more people outside—a lot more people—many with cameras and microphones, plus security guards and men in suits with pistols under their jackets. It took me an hour to work my way out of the mob and across the lawn.

Beyond the White House grounds, there were even more people—people with microphones and cameras, more men in suits with pistols, and DC cops instead of security guards. Then there were the tourists and their children. I viewed the wall of people with dismay. The chances of getting stepped on escalated, and children were the worst when I was small. I never knew what they were going to do or what direction they might decide to move. I cringed as one child cried and stamped his feet while his mother ignored him.

I found myself wishing that I looked like Wen-li. She might be able to grow to her normal size in the middle of a crowd without attracting much notice, but a six-foot-six woman with green hair suddenly appearing in the middle of a crowd was bound to draw people's attention.

It took me another forty minutes to work my way along the base of the fence until I cleared the crowd. I needed to find someplace to change my size. Although my clothing and bag shrunk with me, all of my stuff in the pocket dimension inside the bag didn't. Even if I managed to pull my phone out, it would be almost as large as I was.

A flower bed partially hidden by a tree on the side of the Treasury building gave me enough cover to change my size. I pulled out my phone and called Torbert. We met up and caught a bus.

Torbert and Wen-li pored over the documents, dissecting and analyzing them. Isabella read through them. I was concerned only with the part having to do with me and my property.

I texted my employees, telling them that I was shutting down the business until further notice. The financial hit would be severe, as early summer was my busiest time of the year. I had six crews working, new clients coming on board.

"We have to find another place to stay," I told Miika. "Even with you reinforcing my wards, we can't withstand a concerted attack."

He nodded, knowing I was correct.

During our trip to Pennsylvania, Miika and I talked about our lives back at home. His father was a realm walker who had fallen for a mage on Earth and taken her with him back to Midgard. It happened. While many halflings were the result of mere dalliances, true affection was possible between races. Miika was older than I was, and had traveled more extensively, but he'd spent his early years in Midgard. We had seen mage wars, there and in other realms.

"We can move to my place in Chevy Chase," he said. "If we could get there without detection, it will work, but it can't be fortified even as much as this place."

And there lay the problem. How to get relocated

with all the watchers. Since the President declared the emergency, a small force of soldiers had taken up posts across the street from my gates. The Fairies reported there were more soldiers in the areas surrounding the park.

I had a small fleet of vehicles, but we knew we would be followed if we drove out of the compound, if not arrested. The final declaration of martial law and the order to arrest all illegal aliens had not happened yet, but that was the purpose of the upcoming meeting between the President and Congress.

"I'm betting that Bronski and Nieminen will wait until Congress affirms the President's declaration of martial law, then pull the trigger on that spell," Torbert said. "Any time a full gathering of Congress and the President's Cabinet is called, one Cabinet officer is kept away in case of a disaster." He held up one of the pages from the document. "Bronski and Attorney General Adair will be at Camp David, so Adair will end up as President."

"And Bronski controls Adair," I said.

"We have to find Nieminen," Isabella said.

"That would save a lot of lives," I said, "but it wouldn't change the current situation. We need to kill Bronski and save Adair. We need to prevent the President's speech."

"I'm afraid even that won't change things enough," Torbert said. "That meeting set powerful forces in motion. If everyone in that meeting was convinced to follow Bronski's plan, then they wanted to be convinced. Changing their minds won't be easy."

"There was a man there," I said, "tall with a bit of a stoop as though his back hurt, with gray hair, going bald, and bright blue eyes. Who is that?"

"William Harvey, the President's Chief of Staff. Why?"

"He wasn't convinced. He argued with the President after everyone else left. He said the plan was reckless and poorly conceived. There were two men in military uniforms who didn't act as though they liked the plan, either."

"You don't know their names?"

"No one introduced anyone. They all knew each other."

Wen-li tapped on the keys of Isabella's laptop, then turned the screen toward me. "Any of these men?"

The pictures showed five of the soldiers who had been at the meeting. "They were all there." I pointed at one of the pictures. "That one was very skeptical. One of the men in a business suit said that trying to control non-Humans in the United States was silly because we would just go across the border into Canada or Mexico. But the other soldier who agreed with him isn't in this picture."

Torbert took the laptop and pulled up another picture. "How about him?"

"That's the one."

"General Driscoll, the Marine Corps leader of the Paranormal Strike Force."

"So, what does all that mean?" I asked.

"That there are enough powerful men who might listen if we can free Adair from whatever spell he's under."

CHAPTER 24

As soon as it got dark, we went over the fence and walked to a restaurant. Miika and I left the others there and ran to his place where we got a car.

"You really like fancy cars," I said as we entered the garage.

He laughed. "The BMW we left at the nursery is mine. All of these belong to the house's owner."

"Oh. I thought it was your house."

"It belongs to a friend. She's in another realm right now."

We took a large black Lexus and drove back to the restaurant where we picked up Isabella and the PCU agents. Miika gave each of us a bedroom and, more importantly, from my perspective, a bathroom. It was difficult enough sharing my three-room cottage with four other people, but the small bathroom was totally inadequate for all of us.

"Are you sure the owner won't mind?" I asked. The mansion was huge, the furnishings and decorations obviously expensive. The kitchen alone was larger than my cottage.

"Absolutely," he said. "The owner is a Nephilim, and if she were here, she'd be working with us."

Torbert had selectively contacted colleagues at PCU and other agencies. He arranged a meeting at a restaurant in Silver Spring owned by a friend of his who was a witch. Immediately after arriving at Miika's place, we took two cars and headed out again.

Thankfully, Torbert wasn't any more trusting than I was. He told us frankly that he couldn't be sure everyone he contacted would believe him and take our side. While he and Karen went inside, Miika donned a glamour and took up a post across the street. Isabella leaped on top of the building in her jaguar form and watched from there.

I sort of roamed around, checking side streets, parked cars, and anyplace that looked like a good observation point with a view of the restaurant.

All of the agents Torbert invited showed up. None of them had been told the others would be there. Half an hour after the last invitee entered the restaurant, caravans of cars converged on the place from both directions.

I called Torbert when I saw the first cars coming.

"You've been betrayed," I said when he answered. "Go out the back. Don't let anyone use their phones."

My next call was to Miika. I started to call Isabella, then realized that from her perch she could see the cars coming better than I could.

The first two cars pulled into the parking lot, right by the front door. I walked up to the men getting out of their cars and peppered them with sleepy gas.

As I was turning away, I heard a horrendous crash, followed by two more. An SUV filled with men sat in the middle of the street, looking as though it had run into a wall, but there was nothing there. Two more vehicles had plowed into the first one, creating a terrible mess.

Another car came down the street and slammed on its brakes. Tires squealing, the driver tried to avoid the wreck in front of him and jerked the steering wheel to the right. The rear end of his car clipped the last car in the pileup even as his front wheels hit the curb and flew a few feet into the air. He lost control, and the car skidded into a couple of parked cars.

Miika ran up to me, and we rushed around the side of the building only to find cars entering the parking lot from the side entrance.

He pushed me in the back. "Go! Run! I'll hold them off."

I looked over my shoulder, and saw flame kindle in his hand. The lead car screeched to a stop, and men jumped out of it. Miika hurled a fireball at the car, and it burst into flames. The men dove to the ground. I saw the one closest to me raise a pistol, pointing at Miika.

The noise of the pistol firing coincided with me firing a paintball in the man's direction. Probably none of the Humans saw Miika lean slightly to one side, his movement so slight but so fast. The bullet hit the building behind him. I decided that if he could dodge bullets, I would take his advice. I ran.

Behind me, I heard the swoosh of another fireball, and then another, along with the sound of gunfire. Around the back of the restaurant, I found a man lying face down with a pistol by his hand. His back looked like hamburger. I didn't slow down, hurdling the wall in front of me into someone's backyard. The dog looked startled, but I was over the next wall before it could bark. Two more backyards, then I stopped in the shadow of a large elm tree on the next street.

My phone buzzed and I answered, "Hi, Karen. Where are you?"

She asked, "Are you okay?"

"I'm fine. Where are you?"

"Hiding in a backyard a couple of houses away from the restaurant. It sounds like a war over there."

"Where's Torbert?" I asked.

"He's with me, and so is another PCU agent. Everyone scattered."

"Did everyone get away?"

"I think so. Thanks to Isabella."

"Well, just keep your head down. I'll come for you."

I circled around and came at the restaurant from the same direction some of the cars had come. It wasn't difficult to find my destination. The glow of flames could be seen above the rooflines of the houses between me and the restaurant. I didn't hear anymore gunshots, so I tried Miika's cellphone. No answer, but we all had our phones on buzz.

When I got within sight of the restaurant, I shrank and donned a glamour. Several vehicles were on fire. Men walked around, some hurried from one place to another. A few bodies lay on the ground. In addition to the wreck on the street and burning vehicles in the parking lot, I passed another SUV that looked like it had blown up. I didn't know what kind of spell did that, but it was far beyond my ability.

I didn't care what kind of bullshit Miika tried to feed me about his training. I had seen Elven battle mages in Midgard. Halfling or not, I doubted there were many warriors in Earth's realm who could match him. He had been absolutely calm while facing probably a hundred armed enemies.

Working my way past the battlefield, I checked out backyards until I felt Karen's magic. I snuck up to the gate and grew back to my normal size, then vaulted over the gate. Karen and the others were behind a shed in the far corner of the yard.

I knew the agents were armed, so I let myself glow a little so they could see me. Putting my finger to my lips, I urged them to silence and let the glow fade.

Motioning them to follow me, I scrambled over the wall into the yard behind. One of the men boosted Karen up, and over and I caught her. The two men followed.

We passed through the gate and out to the street, heading away from the scene. The sound of sirens in the distance grew louder as they drew closer. I checked and saw that I had missed one call from Miika, but he had left a message, "I'm back at the car."

"Miika is at the Lexus," I told them as we walked down the street. "It's down this way another block. Do you know where Isabella went?"

"After she took down Kilpatrick," Torbert said, "she jumped back on top of the roof."

That meant she was up there when Miika engaged with the government men.

"We need to hurry," Torbert said, pointing up. A helicopter with a searchlight was heading toward us, probably about a mile away.

Down the street, the black Lexus began rolling toward us with its lights off, and I knew Miika had seen us. He stopped when he reached us, and I pushed Torbert toward the front door, then opened the back. A jaguar lay across the back seat, cleaning her paws, and she gave me a languid yawn.

"Move over," I said, pushing at her. She shifted and scooted to the far side of the car. Karen and the other man jumped in after me. Miika drove off, only turning on the headlights two blocks later.

"What about the car we had to leave at the restaurant?" Torbert asked.

"You weren't the only patrons, were you?" Miika asked in return.

"No, we weren't."

"Don't worry about it. Whoever was after you is going to have a difficult time sorting out the chaos. We'll figure out how to retrieve the car later."

"What happened after we bugged out?" Torbert asked. He turned in his seat to look at Isabella. "Thanks for taking out Kilpatrick."

"Oh, was that the man with the gun?" She gave him a small, lopsided grin. "You're welcome."

"Let's figure out where we're going and what we're doing," I said. "We can talk about the rest later." Considering how fixated Torbert was on following the law, I didn't think that was a good time to tell him Isabella and Miika had slaughtered at least a dozen government agents. That didn't even take into account any injuries or deaths of the men riding in the cars that wrecked or were incinerated.

"Back to your house," Torbert said. "We need to see who escaped."

"Pretty much everyone who went into the restaurant, I think," I said. "I didn't see any of the men who met with you when I passed through the parking lot. The question is, did you have only one informant?"

The other PCU agent was introduced as Tom Edwards. He appeared to be older than Karen, but younger than Dave, and I didn't detect any magic in him. As we rode, he told us that Kilpatrick hung back when the group escaped out the back door, then followed with his gun drawn. He declared them all under arrest for treason. That was when his world collapsed under two hundred pounds of jaguar.

"I didn't see any of the other men run toward the cars," Isabella said.

"We did gain some very valuable information from the meeting," Torbert told us. "Two of the men I invited are with the Secret Service, and we have the travel plans for Bronski and Adair on Thursday. I'm not sure we have the manpower to do anything about them, though."

Isabella chuckled.

"We have to be careful," I said. "We need Adair alive and healthy."

"And we need Bronski dead," Miika said. "We don't know what kind of spells he used on Attorney General Adair. As long as Bronski's alive, we have to worry about latent spells that could be triggered by Goddess knows what."

I completely agreed with that. Bronski may not have been a strong mage, but he was a very clever and unscrupulous one.

By morning, all but one of the government agents at the meeting had contacted Torbert. And as crazy and loud as the battle had been, not a breath of it was heard on TV or the internet news. Isabella found several accounts of it on social media, however, including a fifteen-minute video taken from the second floor of a house about half a block from the restaurant. We all clustered around.

"Holy..." Karen breathed. The video showed Miika casually tossing fireballs and blocking bullets as though he was playing a game. Isabella seemed to materialize from the air, landing on the roof of an SUV, tearing the driver's door off its hinges, and then diving inside. I was thankful there wasn't any sound. She sprang out of the vehicle after a couple of minutes, but none of the men inside ever emerged.

The fight lasted only about five minutes, then Miika suddenly vanished. Isabella leaped from the parking lot to the top of a car, then to the top of the building, and never reappeared. The rest of the video showed the aftermath with the stunned FBI agents stumbling around.

"So, what's our next step?" I asked. "We have today and tomorrow to try and find Aleksi Nieminen. Dave, do you think Bronski is smart enough to be doing all this on his own, or is Nieminen keeping him on a tight leash and pulling his strings?"

It was Karen who answered. "Clever? Yes. Smart? Not really, and definitely not a strategic thinker. If you tell him to go to Baltimore, and that there are obstacles in the way, he'll figure it out. But if you asked him whether he should target Baltimore or Richmond, he'd be stumped."

"What are you thinking?" Torbert asked me.

"Can any of your technology listen in on Bronski's phone calls? We need to find out where he is and keep an eye on him. Use him to try and find Nieminen." I turned my eyes toward Miika. "Then when Bronski and Adair leave town, we ambush them and take out Bronski? At that point, we have to hope that Adair understands what's happened, and that it matters."

Torbert nodded. "That makes sense. But if we don't find Nieminen, the risk is still there."

"It would make things more difficult for Nieminen to take control of the country, but the chaos, the fear, the leadership vacuum would still be there," Isabella said. "Saving Adair is only important for turning things around. If the President and his advisors continue down the path they're on, it won't matter that we've saved their asses."

"We have to try," I said. I gestured at the screen. "That will look like a picnic if the government thinks they can take on the paranormal community.

Nieminen is a fool. Human mages might have been atop the food chain when we were all hidden, but starting a mage war is completely insane."

"I agree," Miika said. "He has no idea what he's getting into, and the power from a blood-magic fetish will just unify white mages against him."

"You've seen mage wars?" Isabella asked.

Miika and I both nodded. "Elves are rather arrogant," Miika said. "The thirst for power is very strong in some people."

CHAPTER 25

The group decided that Dave and Karen needed to stay at the house because they were too recognizable. Too many of the people hunting us knew them personally. Miika and I could disguise ourselves by donning a glamour, so we would be the ones going out and trying to gather information and track down Nieminen.

Edwards went to work like he normally did on Tuesday mornings. He rigged his cell phone to send an alarm to Torbert if he was arrested. If he could get close to Bronski, the plan was for him to plant a tracking chip on the new PCU chief.

I wasn't entirely comfortable depending on technology, but I didn't have even the small laboratory at my cottage. I mentioned that to Miika and Karen, and after some discussion, we decided to try and get me into my Georgetown townhouse.

We took a car I hadn't ridden in yet—a flashy red two-seat sports car. With a laugh, Miika said the best way to be inconspicuous was to be conspicuous. He donned a glamour of a man past middle age, half bald with white hair. My glamour was a blonde with large breasts in her mid-twenties. He dropped me off in the shopping district on M Street.

I wandered through a couple of shops, changing my glamour first to a woman ten years older, then later I added another ten years and fifty pounds, with far more conservative clothing. I couldn't detect anyone watching me while I walked the five blocks to my house.

Miika had driven past the house twice, passing in front, turning down the side street, then coming back the same way several minutes later. He called and told me he hadn't seen anyone who looked as though they were watching the house.

I walked past, trying to see anything that looked out of place, feeling for magic of any kind. Turning the corner, I walked into a shadow and blurred my image as I backed against the wall. Practically holding my breath, I waited for about twenty minutes. No one came to see where I had gone, and I didn't see anyone else on the street. In a single motion, I vaulted over the wall into my back courtyard.

My wards were undisturbed, though some trace residuals told me that at least one magic user had tried to get in. Once I was in the house, I called Miika, and he left to drive by the nursery and see what kind of force Bronski had set to watching us there. We hoped that no one knew we had left, or that all of us had left, but I doubted the people watching were that stupid.

I spent two hours in my lab, creating some magical trackers and a scrying stone keyed to Nieminen's blood. I also created something that I hoped might help locate the statue. I had no idea whether it would work, but figured it was worth a try. I used my own blood in the spell, something that skirted the edges of what the Goddess permitted.

Pocketing all my work, I crept out of the rooftop hatch and crossed roofs until I reached a tree between two buildings and climbed down. Miika picked me up, and we went back to his place.

Edwards called just before noon and told Torbert that another of the men who escaped the restaurant managed to stick a tracker on Bronski's suit coat. Edwards transmitted the tracker's address, and we input it to an app on my and Miika's cell phones.

We drove downtown and left the car in a parking garage. The tracking app showed that Bronski was at the Department of Justice, near the National Mall, which made sense. That's where Adair's office was. I checked the GPS on my phone to make sure I knew where we were going. That map triggered a thought, so I checked a couple of other things.

"Miika, if you draw a circle eighteen hundred and twenty-four yards from the Department of Justice, it includes both the Capitol and the White House, not to mention most of the main government buildings."

"So?"

"That was the diameter of that crater out in Arlington. And not only the White House," I continued, "it would reach the river. We'll have a national lake instead of a National Mall."

He looked over my shoulder at my phone. "That has to be where Aleksi plans to hold his ritual."

"That's my guess. The only good thing about it is that demons hate water, so we might not have the same problems afterward as we did in Arlington."

He snorted a laugh. "Trying to see the silver lining?"

I shrugged. "If it wasn't for a blood mage trying to take over the world, doing away with that weird, dysfunctional government has its appeal."

"You do have a point. So, how do we get into this Department of Justice?"

Using the same kinds of glamour to conceal our identities as we used before, we found the building and walked all the way around it. The tracking app consistently told us that Bronski was in the building.

"Or at least the tracking chip is," Miika said.

I called Torbert.

"How do you get into DOJ?" he repeated my question back to me. "You don't, at least right now. Security there is as tight as the Capitol or the White House. There is a café inside, but I'm not sure it's open to the public."

I heard Karen's voice in the background, and Torbert said, "Hang on a minute."

Karen took the phone and said, "There is a secret system of tunnels under the city that connect the White House with the Capitol and a number of other places. Security is tight, but there's one access point you might be able to sneak into."

She went on to tell me about an entrance to the secret complex through a hotel near the White House.

"Okay, where in the hotel do we go?"

"Well, I've never been there," she said. "I just know it's there. We'll have to find it."

"No problem," Miika said when I hung up. "We just look for the nasty-looking men with automatic rifles standing next to a door that says, 'no admittance'."

I pulled the piece of lapis lazuli I had spelled out of my pocket. "I don't feel the statue, and this scrying stone I spelled to search out Nieminen isn't reacting either. I don't think it would do us much good to try and use the hidden tunnels right now."

Miika shook his head. "I agree with you. My understanding, though, is this is only a place of work. Bronski and Adair should be leaving sometime. Shall we simply wait for them?"

That sounded good to me.

While I watched the building, or more accurately, watched the app on my phone, Miika hiked down the street to a food truck and brought back some takeout.

Even after seventy years in Earth's realm, the unhealthy nature of a Polish sausage with sauerkraut and brown mustard on white bread made me cringe a little, but it tasted so good. We sat on a bus stop bench and ate while we waited. It was a huge building, and occasionally the app showed Bronski moving around inside, so I assumed it was working.

At about four o'clock Miika said, "He's moving."

I looked down at my phone and saw the dot that symbolized Bronski moving from the middle of the building to the edge of the diagram symbolizing the building. We jumped up and hurried around the building. A limousine pulled up to the curb in front of one of the doors.

"Go get the car," I said. "I'll follow them." I looked around and no one was paying attention to us. I changed my glamour to that of a jogger. Miika took off in the direction of the parking garage and I waited.

Bronski and Adair came out of the building and got in the limo. I knew it couldn't go very fast in downtown traffic, so I followed them, sprinting when I needed to, but conscious that I needed to run slow enough not to attract attention.

I had done some research attempting to educate myself about the U.S. government—how it worked, and who the key players were. Adair was a wealthy lawyer who became a politician, then he was appointed Attorney General. He owned a house in a wealthy enclave not too far from my place in Georgetown. Miika caught up with us as the limo turned onto Massachusetts Avenue, and I jumped in.

"I think they're headed to Adair's house in Kalorama," I said.

"Maybe we can take them there."

"I don't know. There's a car ahead of them and

218

one behind, with four men in each. I assume they're guarding him."

It turned out that I was right. The limo and the other two cars pulled into a gated driveway, and the gate closed.

But as soon as we turned onto that street, a unique stench of blood magic mixed with demon essence assaulted me and I gagged. It was far more powerful than what I had sensed at either Weber's home or laboratory. I pulled out the scrying stone, and found it was unnaturally warm.

"It's here," I said.

Miika turned toward me. "What's here?"

"The statue. The jaguar statue. Can't you sense it?"

He shook his head. "You seem to always know when magic is around, and what kind of magic it is. You asked if I am a battle mage, but most Elves would never associate that with a halfling."

I thought about it. I had always been able to identify magic, both its type and strength. Identifying Bronski as a mage and Karen as a witch was automatic, even though she was stronger than he was.

"I guess so," I answered him as I pulled out my phone and called Isabella. When she answered, I said, "We found the statue and Aleksi Nieminen."

We left Isabella with a pair of binoculars in Rock Creek Park where she could watch Adair's house. Miika and I stopped by a market and picked up food, then went back to the Chevy Chase house where I took a shower and cooked dinner. After we ate, Miika delivered a large, uncooked roast to Isabella, who planned to spend the night in the park.

That evening, Torbert briefed us on what to expect.

"Usually, the President takes a helicopter to Camp David," Torbert said, "but my sources say that Adair is going to drive. He evidently doesn't like to fly." He showed us a picture of a car on Isabella's laptop. "Does this look like the car they were using?"

We nodded. What I knew about limousines could be stuffed in an acorn.

"That is one of the most heavily armored and protected vehicles in the world," Torbert said. "In addition to ballistic armoring and special glass six inches thick, it has a sealed cabin with an independent air supply, infrared smoke-screen and oil-slick deployment capabilities, and tear gas dispensers. I don't know what kind of magic you plan to use, but cracking that car is going to be difficult. It's basically a rolling fortress. The escort vehicles are specially armored SUVs, so they aren't easy to attack either."

Thursday morning, Isabella reported that Bronski and Adair once again set out in the limo. When I checked the app on my phone, I discovered they weren't on a route toward downtown, but rather heading north on Massachusetts Avenue.

Miika and I jumped in the sports car and managed to tuck in behind Adair's motorcade as it took the beltway to the I-270 ramp toward Frederick. In addition to the armored limo carrying Adair and Bronski, there were two SUVs ahead, and three behind. Where the road was wider, one of the trailing SUVs pulled alongside the limo.

I pointed out a helicopter flying above the convoy. "That helicopter may be a problem. They'll be able to see anything we do," Miika said.

I called Torbert and told him what we had seen. "They are evidently going up to Camp David today," I told Torbert. "Isabella said that Nieminen wasn't with them when they left. Can you supply some backup for her? You need to track him when he leaves Adair's house."

"You do realize," Torbert said, "if Nieminen decides to use the statue from where he is, he'll not only take out the richest power brokers in Washington, but half of the foreign embassies in town. And your friend Isabella is right at ground zero."

"Are you always so cheerful in the morning?" I asked.

"It's my job to try and anticipate disasters."

"What I can't figure out," I said, "is how that thing in Arlington happened without taking Nieminen and the statue along with the rest of Pentagon City."

"Well, let me know if you do figure it out," Torbert responded. "Every time I think about that, I get a headache."

We followed Adair's limo to Fredrick, Maryland, and then onto the road to Catoctin Mountain Park, where Camp David was located. At that point, I was pretty sure Bronski wouldn't deviate from the plan I'd overheard at the White House.

I told Miika, "Torbert says we won't be able to get within miles of Camp David due to their security. The GPS on my phone won't even show a route to Camp David."

"So, what do you want me to do?"

"Pass them. Let's get ahead of them and find a good spot for an ambush."

He grinned. "Sounds like a good idea to me."

I did expect him to find a reasonable place to pass, not do it on a corner, whipping the sports car back into the right lane seconds before we splattered on the grill of a truck. I spent the next twenty minutes debating with myself whether I wanted a policeman to stop us for speeding.

Shortly after entering the park, Miika braked hard for a corner that turned out to be sharper than he anticipated.

"Pull over," I shouted, waving my hands. "Pull over."

He finally did. "What?"

"Find a good place to hide the car. That corner was perfect."

That got me a raised eyebrow, then he puckered his lips, looked at me kind of sideways, and said, "Yes, you're probably right."

I jumped out and trotted back the way we'd come, while he went in search of a hiding place for the car. A glance at the tracking app on my phone showed Bronski a little less than ten minutes behind us.

The road wound through tall trees growing close to the road, and any car would have to slow down for that corner. It had been raining—more of an on-and-off drizzle—and I thought I had exactly the spell I needed to set up our ambush.

Standing about fifty feet before the road curved, I drew a rune in the air and said a Word. The pavement turned very shiny. A second rune spell dropped the temperature of the road and secured the first spell.

Miika came trotting down the road toward me.

"Watch out!" I shouted. "Get off the road."

He smiled and waved at me, and veered to the side of the road, but he'd gone too far. His feet flew out from under him, and he landed hard on his back. I ran to him, careful to stay on the dirt shoulder and not step on the pavement.

"What did you do?" he asked with a moan as he rolled over. He tried to push himself to his hands and knees, and one hand slid away from him.

"Just slide toward me," I said.

He ended up scooting off the road on his butt, like a baby who hadn't learned to crawl, and I tried not to laugh.

"I may not be a battle mage," I told him, "but I know enough rune magic to freeze and thaw water. When they brake for that corner, they're going to discover they don't have any traction."

I showed him the thickets on both sides of the road where we could hide. "Have you figured out how you're going to open up that car?" I asked him. Simply destroying the car and those inside wouldn't be difficult, but we needed Adair alive. I pulled out my bow and strung it, then drew my paintball gun.

"Magic," he said, and winked at me.

CHAPTER 26

The lead SUV came into the corner and braked as the driver turned the wheels. The vehicle continued straight without losing any speed until it crashed into the trees. The following SUV crashed into it. The presidential limo continued the trend. Sort of a 'crash', 'Crash', 'CRASH'.

All three armored vehicles were so heavy that the smashup was spectacularly destructive.

Miika sketched a rune, and as the limo passed us, he spoke a Word. The SUV following the limo crashed into nothing, just as the FBI SUV had done outside the restaurant in Silver Spring. The two following vehicles smashed into it.

Awestruck, I said, "You have to teach me that spell."

"Glad to," Miika answered. "It's an air spell that condenses the molecules of the air into a solid wall."

He began to sketch another rune, an incredibly complex one, but I wasn't able to watch him finish. Some of the men in the last three SUVs staggered out of their vehicles, and I shot them with sleepy-gas paintballs. Sliding out onto the roadway, I fired more paintballs into the passenger compartments. I put the gun back in my bag and nocked an arrow to my bow.

We waited and watched the three vehicles that had piled up in the trees. I kept glancing up, waiting for the helicopter to fly over, but didn't see it. Miika still hid in the brush on the side of the road.

I crossed the road and entered the woods, working my way around so that I could come at the crash from the other side. I reached a place where I could see inside the cars. The two SUVs were a total loss. The airbags had deployed and obscured my sight to an extent, and I didn't see any movement.

Sneaking closer, crouching low so that anyone inside the cars would have to look down to see me, I made my way to the first vehicle. One of its doors had popped partially open, so I fired a couple of paintballs inside.

Moving to the next SUV, sandwiched between the SUV in front and the limo behind, I had a very bad feeling. The massive limo had some damage, but its impact had really crunched the second SUV. I reached out with my senses, and felt four sources of life energy inside, but I could tell all four were injured.

A sizzling sound, like frying bacon, grabbed my attention. The sound was followed by a weird smell. I looked up and saw Miika standing behind the limo, an expression of intense concentration on his face. He held his arms in front of him, forming a circle with his hands, and white-hot energy poured from that circle toward the limo.

Backing away from the cars, I circled around so that I could see. The energy was focused on the back window, and the glass appeared to be melting.

The limo's back door on the side away from me suddenly swung open, and Bronski jumped out. A silvery ball of energy flew toward Miika, who was slow to react. The energy ball struck him a glancing blow, spinning him around and sending him flying a few feet. He hit the pavement and slid on the ice.

I drew my bow and loosed, the arrow piercing Bronski's chest. His eyes bulged, and he made a strangled noise. Staggering backward, he turned his eyes toward me as he fell. I nocked another arrow and sidled around the back of the limo, ready for Bronski to retaliate, but also trying to keep an eye on the open limo door.

Bronski lay on his back, staring at the sky, and I relaxed slightly. The front door of the limo popped open, and the driver rolled out. He raised a pistol and fired. I heard a popping sound to my left, and I moved to my right as I pulled and loosed my arrow. It hit the shooter in the upper left side of his chest just as he fired again. I ducked behind the limo and heard the popping sound of the bullet passing above me. A scrabbling noise came from the inside of the limo, and then the sound of a second person scraping along the pavement outside. "You okay?" I heard, then a strained response, "Yeah. Watch your ass. She's damned good with that bow."

I took that as my cue to put away my bow and draw the paintball gun again. Lying prone under the limo, I fired five paintballs, hoping to get lucky, or at least sow some confusion. Rising to a crouch, I sprinted past the two wrecked SUVs into the woods, then looked back from a hiding place behind a tree.

I got lucky. The man struck by an arrow also had a pink splotch on his side and lay still. The other man had tried to run, but the ice on the road was as unforgiving with him as it had been with Miika. The guy lost his pistol when he fell and slid, so I simply walked around the end of the ice and approached him from the other side of the road.

His face radiated hate as he looked up at me. I shot him twice with paintballs and watched him fall asleep.

From where I stood, I could see into the limo. Adair peered out at me, fear and anger warring on his face.

"Mister Adair," I called, "It would be better if you

got out on the other side of the car. I'm afraid the road here is too slick to stand."

"Who the hell are you?" he shouted. "Where are we? What the hell is going on?"

Rather than answer, I skated over to where Miika lay. I held my breath as I bent down, but he was breathing, and his heart was beating strongly. I couldn't see any obvious wounds. The spell Bronski used looked a lot like a spell I knew, using a rune to draw energy from the world and coalescing it into a ball that could be thrown. It was a minor weapon compared to the fireballs and heat lance I'd seen Miika use, but that kind of power was far beyond me.

Leaving him there, I slid the few feet to the edge of the road and looked back at the wrecked cars. Adair had taken my advice and stood by the open back door of the limo.

"What is going on?" he asked.

I motioned at Bronski's body. "Alan Bronski is a blood mage, if you know what that is. He cast a spell on you, a compulsion spell, and turned you into his puppet. You named him head of the PCU after he assassinated the agents above him, and then had you convince the President that paranormal beings are conspiring to take over the government. Does any of that sound familiar?"

He stared at me with narrowed eyes, then shook his head and put his hands over his face. When he lowered his hands a couple of minutes later, he said, "And who are you? How did we get here?"

"The President is speaking to a joint session of Congress tonight. You are the designated survivor on your way to Camp David. As for me? I'm the one Bronski accused of leading a conspiracy by non-Humans to enslave you all. Which is pretty insulting.

What the hell am I supposed to do with six billion slaves?"

He looked confused, which was understandable. I pulled out my phone. "Would you like to speak with David Torbert of the PCU? Jim Roberts is in the hospital, and my understanding is that Torbert is his second in command?"

"Yes, that would be correct." He looked around at the trees and all the wrecked vehicles. "What about the director of the FBI?"

"Torbert said that the entire leadership was unavailable for one reason or another. I think a couple of them are dead, a couple in the hospital. Some are just missing." I handed him my phone.

He and Torbert spoke for about twenty minutes. I used the time to pull Miika off the road into some shade. I retrieved a water bottle from one of the SUVs and tried to pour a little in his mouth. Other than that, I had no idea what to do.

I knew some of the government men needed medical care, but I didn't know if any or all of them were willing participants in Bronski's conspiracy. I hadn't shed a tear for those who tried to arrest Torbert and Karen. Elves didn't overthink moral choices the way Humans were prone to. In any case, I wasn't a healer, so I doubted I could do much for someone who was injured.

Adair walked over and handed me my phone. "Agent Torbert wants to speak with you."

"Kellana," Torbert said when I answered, "we're going to get a helicopter out to you. Adair says there are injured people there?"

"Yes, there was a big car wreck, and one guy took an arrow. Everyone is sleeping now. But I don't know if a helicopter can find us. There was one that followed the convoy from DC, but Miika did something, and I haven't seen or heard the helicopter since. Miika's unconscious, so I can't ask him about it." I thought about it. "Can't you send some people from Camp David? I was under the impression there's a permanent staff there."

"There is. I'll do that."

"Have them send a doctor. I don't know what to do with the people who are hurt. What did you and Adair talk about?"

"He's put me in charge of the PCU. Got a lot to do, call you later."

A convoy of SUVs, two ambulances, and a couple of cars came down the road about forty minutes later. Two state police cars showed up from the DC direction twenty minutes after that. They had to cut two of the men in the middle SUV out of it. There were broken bones, cracked heads, and numerous minor injuries, but thankfully, no one died except Bronski.

I tried to slip away with Miika, but they caught me. He was just too heavy to run with. They took us to Camp David and shut us up together in a bedroom in one of the lodges. They didn't take our phones away from us, though, and to my surprise, they didn't find Miika's car. They also didn't take my bag, where I had all my weapons and Miika's sword.

He woke up about two o'clock in the afternoon. Although he was a little shaky at first, he recovered quickly. We took the hinges off the door, walked out, put the door back in place, and locked it again. A twenty-minute run brought us to where the car was hidden.

I hung on so hard that my hands hurt as he drove back to DC going well over one hundred miles an hour most of the way. He must have done something to hide us, as we passed several police cars, and none of them noticed us.

We pulled into the driveway in Chevy Chase about four o'clock. Several cars I didn't recognize sat in the driveway or parked out on the street. When we walked in, I saw several of the men from the meeting at the restaurant. There were several TVs in the house, and every one of them was tuned to a news channel. All the news was about the President's speech and the threat of the 'paranormals', as the media liked to call anyone who wasn't Human.

Riots and lynchings had erupted in parts of the United States, and there were rumors of a battle in Mexico between witches and government soldiers. Depending on which channel the TV was tuned to, the witches were either winning or losing.

I barely had time to eat something when Isabella called. "Nieminen is leaving Adair's house," she said. "I'm following him."

"Saddle up," Torbert called out. "Everyone knows what they're supposed to do."

A few minutes of hectic activity later, Miika and I stood alone with Karen in the middle of the kitchen.

"We're supposed to follow Isabella and Nieminen," Karen said.

CHAPTER 27

Aleksi Nieminen drove to a parking garage near DuPont Circle and left his rental car there. Isabella parked a few cars away from his and tracked him by scent into the Metro. She lost him when he evidently boarded a train.

Karen took my phone and advised Isabella, "Head for the W Hotel near the White House. Take the Red Line to Metro Center."

She handed my phone back. "He parked more than a mile away from the Justice building. I guess he doesn't want to walk after he blows up the city." She went back to talking on her phone.

I checked a map and found that the parking garage would indeed be beyond the circle of destruction.

"Is that where I should go?" Miika, who was driving, asked.

"Hell, no," I said. "If we don't stop him, we won't need a car. Get as close to the hotel as possible."

While we were parking, Isabella called again and said she had picked up the scent on the train platform at Metro Center. Her nose must be phenomenal, I thought. I never would have been able to separate the smell of one person on a train platform. Actually, the whole idea of getting my nose that close to a train platform made me rather nauseous.

I checked the time when we reached the hotel. We still had three hours until the scheduled start of the President's speech.

Isabella stood in the lobby waiting for us. "He went to the Justice Department and just waltzed in the door. They wouldn't let me in, so I came here to wait for you."

Karen pointed to a door marked, 'Authorized Personnel Only'. "That's how we get in."

Four men in suits approached us. I could tell they had pistols under their jackets. Karen pulled out her identification and held it up. The four men did the same.

"Agent Wen-li?" one of them asked. "I'm Agent Patterson, Secret Service. This is Agent Clark, Agent Nugent, and Agent Jones."

"These are the contractors working with us," Karen said. "Miika Apthenir, Kellana Rogirsdottir, and Doctor Isabella Cortez. Ms. Rogirsdottir and Dr. Cortez know the suspect on sight. Mr. Apthenir is a mage. If we run into a problem, please try not to get between them and the problem."

All four nodded. "We've worked with paranormals before," Patterson said.

He led the way to the door Isabella pointed out, slid a card through a scanner, then put his eye to a round, hollow bump on the wall. The door clicked and he pulled it open. We walked down a hallway to another door where he did the same thing. That door opened onto a stairwell, and we headed down.

The Humans' footfalls on the metal steps echoed loudly as we descended twelve flights of stairs. Turning onto the final flight, I saw two soldiers with automatic rifles standing on either side of the door at the bottom. I surreptitiously sketched a rune and noticed that Miika did the same.

When we reached the bottom, Patterson held up his identification and said, "Secret Service."

In a voice with no inflection whatsoever, one of

the soldiers said, "You are not authorized."

Miika and I said the same Word simultaneously, and then the soldiers started firing. The noise was deafening in the closed space. Isabella ducked, while Karen and the Secret Service agents all dove to the floor, drawing their pistols.

I exchanged a glance with Miika and said, "I'll do it." I drew my paintball gun, and he jerked a short nod.

The soldiers ran out of bullets and reached for replacement magazines. I dissolved my spell and fired. Pink splashes on the soldiers' chests turned into a pink fog, and then they both slumped to the floor.

"Are they—" one of the agents started.

"Asleep," I said. "They'll wake up in about four hours. The range of this gun isn't very far, though."

Another agent asked, "Is that stuff for sale?"

I gave him a wink. "If we all survive this, buy me a drink and we'll talk about it."

Patterson unlocked the door, and we emerged onto a platform overlooking a pair of train tracks. He motioned to his right. "The Justice Department is that way, about five hundred yards."

"What's in the other direction?" Isabella asked.

"The White House."

"Do you know where Nieminen might be going?" she asked. "He's been in and out of the building fairly regularly, so I assume he has a place he plans to work."

Karen answered. "Attorney General Adair told Torbert to find a mage named Susan O'Shaughnessy who has been working with Bronski. Her office is on the third floor."

Isabella and I exchanged a look.

"Can you find out if she has another space? A laboratory or storage room, or something like that?" Isabella asked.

"Maybe when we get above ground," one of the agents said. "We're too far below ground to get any service here."

"He won't be doing any rituals in a third-floor office," I said. "He'll want something more private. We don't even know how long the ritual takes. He may need to start on it hours ahead of time."

"You know what bothers me?" Karen asked. "We don't know who the bad guys are. Some of the people trying to kill us are agents I've had a drink with, like Kilpatrick."

I nodded, thinking of the Secret Service agents injured in the car wrecks near Camp David. "You have to assume that anyone who gets in our way needs to be dealt with. Like I told Torbert, this is a war. Just remember Arlington. Everyone, including us, will die if Nieminen completes his plan."

Patterson gave me a long look. "If we fail, we get another Arlington?"

"Yes," Isabella said. "Maybe worse. That was his first attempt to use the artifact. We don't know what he learned from that, or what he's learned since."

"Let us know when we're getting close," I said. "I'd prefer to avoid any repeats of that scene under the W."

Patterson looked between Miika and me and nodded.

The tunnel didn't run straight, but rather took a long curve from the hotel to Justice. Gradually, the platform at Justice came into sight. I took the lead, and we hugged the tunnel walls to break up our outlines and hide our presence as long as possible. My vision was far better than the Humans', and better than Miika's.

The platform at the hotel had been flat and empty, with not even a bench for someone to sit and wait. But there appeared to be a wall along the tunnel between the Justice platform and the walkway.

"Agent Patterson," I said, "have any of you ever been through here before?"

He motioned to someone behind him, and Agent Clark came forward.

"There's some sort of wall across the end of this walkway where it meets the platform," I said. "Is that how it's always been?"

He thought a moment, then said, "No. None of the platforms have a barrier or any kind of gate. Only this railing on the side of the platform." He reached out and touched the safety rail to our left.

"I'll go," Miika said. "Set a protective ward."

He sketched a rune, another very complex one, said a Word, drew his sword, and set off down the tunnel. I set the same ward I had used under the hotel. We waited.

Miika sidled down the tunnel with his back to the wall and a glamour blurring his image. I watched as he worked his way close to the platform and reached the barrier.

A bright light flashed forth from the barrier, enveloping Miika. He responded by sketching runes in the air over his head with both hands. Bright yellow bursts of energy shot from between his hands, illuminating a ward in front of him as it absorbed and dissipated each burst. After a few minutes, the ward shimmered, faltered, and collapsed. A machinegun opened fire, but another burst of energy flashed forth from Miika's hands, something behind the barrier exploded, and the gun fell silent.

Miika jumped over the barrier brandishing his sword. I heard faint screams, then silence. Miika stood at the barrier and signaled us forward.

We climbed over the concrete barrier and found six bodies dressed in military combat uniforms. A machinegun on a tripod lay in the middle of the platform, looking as though it had exploded.

"There was a trap spell and a ward," he told me.

"Set by Nieminen?" Isabella asked.

He shrugged. "Him or another mage. No way of knowing." He leaned toward me. "There is nothing to pull energy from down here except the earth itself. If there are more such obstacles, it will be difficult."

I understood what he meant. The energy he used to break the ward came from his own life energy. Reaching in my bag, I pulled out a grapefruit and a chuck of beef jerky. He devoured them and gave me a grateful smile. It wouldn't replace all the energy he expended, but it would help.

Patterson opened the door, and we filed inside the building. We climbed twelve flights of stairs to another door, and Patterson again opened it. The two guards on the other side were disarmed and handcuffed. I shot a paintball that put them to sleep.

Karen checked her phone. "Hey, we have a problem." We waited while she called Torbert. After a couple of minutes, she set the phone to speaker and held it out. We all clustered around.

"The Army has jumped the gun," Torbert said. "They've moved troops into the city and set up defensive perimeters around the White House, Pentagon, Capitol, and most of the main department headquarters, including Justice and the FBI. They're blocking both entrance and exit, so we can't get Adair into the Capitol."

"So, even if we stop Nieminen, the President will still go ahead with his speech and the Congressional vote," Isabella said. "We can save their fucking lives, and they'll sign our death warrants. Why do we bother?"

None of the Humans, even Karen, would meet my eyes, or look at Isabella or Miika.

"Because it's the right thing to do," I said into the silence. "The same reason I agreed to help you find that damned statue."

Isabella bit her lip, then grabbed Karen's phone. "Saying 'I can't' isn't good enough, Torbert. People are dying already. Get your ass in gear and get it done. Cut the power or something."

A moment of silence was followed by Torbert saying, "Yes, ma'am. I'm on it."

"Okay," I said, "Where do we look?" It was a big building, and time was winding down.

"Where are we?" Isabella asked.

"In the sub-basement," Patterson said.

"Well, let's start here."

We set off down a long hallway with Miika in the lead. I extended my senses, trying to identify whether any life energy existed behind the doors we passed. It appeared that most of the rooms were used for storage, and I didn't expect many people to be down there after working hours.

The scrying stone heated up the moment we emerged from the stairwell. Nieminen was somewhere close, but for all the stone could tell me he might be six floors above me.

The building was huge, and after scouting down only one hall longer than a soccer field, I knew we didn't have a chance of searching it all in time. I called the group together.

"This is too slow. I'm sorry, but we can't wait for you. Miika and I will go ahead." I knew that Isabella could keep up with us in her jaguar form over a short distance, but I didn't know about her endurance. She obviously wasn't worried about that, as she changed and snarled at me. I turned and ran.

I soon outdistanced Miika, which I realized was due in part to his halfling heritage, but also due to the difference in how men and women were built. My legs were longer. Isabella kept up with me for a while, but gradually fell behind.

I was racing down a hallway in the middle of the building when the stench of the statue hit me like an avalanche. I stumbled and almost fell, my stomach rebelling. Skidding to a stop, I cast about me and realized the sense of the foulness came from above me. We were on the wrong level. I leaned over, my arms wrapped around me, and fought the urge to vomit. The scrying stone was almost too hot to touch.

Isabella caught up to me, rubbed against me, then changed. "What's the matter? Are you okay?" She leaned down, trying to see my face.

I didn't trust myself to talk, but I pointed toward the ceiling.

"We're on the wrong level? Crap." She straightened up and then grabbed my arm. "Come on. We passed an elevator in that last corridor."

The farther I got from the statue, the better I felt. We were almost to the cross-corridor when we met Miika.

"We need to go up," I said. But when we reached

238

the elevator, we discovered it didn't work. We went searching for another one or a stairwell.

Coming around a corner, we ran into Karen and the Secret Service agents.

"We need the next level," I said. "I can feel it up there."

Patterson informed us that half of the elevators were out of service due to a project to replace them all. We finally found a stairway near one corner of the building. We climbed the steps, and I stopped at the top, trying to get my bearings and identify where in the massive building I had felt the statue.

Karen consulted a map she had on her phone, and said, "This way, I think. It's part of the library."

It took us about ten minutes to reach the room she identified. As soon as we turned down the corridor, I had no doubt. Bracing myself and taking a deep breath, I said, "It's here."

CHAPTER 28

We approached a double metal door, and everyone spread out around it in the hallway. I reached out and tried to open the door, but it was locked. Miika sketched a rune, and when he spoke the Word, the metal of the handle crumbled into dust. I stuck my finger in the hole it left and pulled the door open.

Isabella slipped past me into the room, and Miika followed her. I drew my sword and trailed after them.

I found myself in a large room with shelves filled with paper file folders. All the lights were off, but a glow deeper in the room provided enough light for us to see clearly.

I checked the time. The President was scheduled to speak at nine o'clock, and it was five minutes after eight. Most of the people allowed into the Capitol would be there, and the President would show up around eight forty-five.

Quietly sneaking through the room, I heard chanting in a language I didn't recognize. I laid a hand on Isabella's back, and we slowly crept forward.

A nude woman, who I assumed was Susan O'Shaughnessy, lay on a wooden table in an open area in the middle of the room. Silver spikes pinned her wrists to the table, and more silver spikes through the hollows of her ankles held her spread legs. Her eyes were open, and her face showed no signs that she was in any kind of discomfort.

Surrounding the table were five candle stands in the shape of a pentagram, linked by a black line. Three feet farther out were five more candles, connected by a white line that I assumed was salt. A circle, also drawn with salt, ringed everything. A naked man wearing a cloak stood chanting in the space between the two pentagrams.

Nieminen had used a mage for his spell in Arlington, and another one to summon a demon. As far as I could tell, O'Shaughnessy was still intact. There wasn't any blood on her torso, though she was marked with symbols drawn with ashes. She was obviously either drugged or bespelled, as she gazed with adoration on the man who planned to murder her. If she was in her right mind, her crucifixion would have hurt like hell.

A golden statue of a jaguar stood gleaming in the candlelight between the woman's thighs. Three hundred pounds of gold translated to a statue about a foot high and maybe two and a half feet long.

I took a strong hold of Isabella's hide, but she seemed to have learned from her experience jumping into a mage's circle.

Nieminen didn't react to our presence, but he was busy, and I figured he hadn't seen us yet. Miika began to draw one of his complex runes in the air, and I moved a little away and behind him. I wasn't sure what he had in mind, but the last place I wanted to be when the magic started flying was between a battle mage and a blood mage. For the first time, it struck me that we might stop Nieminen's plans and still die. The amount of power building in the room was immense.

Miika stopped. The rune hung in the air, complex, beautiful, and terrible, glowing with an inner fire. He took a deep breath, raised his hands into the air, and spoke the Word that activated it.

The room exploded, and as I flew through the air, I had time to think that I probably shouldn't have been standing so close.

I hit one of the metal shelves, hard enough to drive all the air from my lungs and feel a couple of ribs crack. Luckily, the shelves weren't bolted down, the weight of their contents holding them in place. The shelf tipped and fell, and I landed on top of it in a cloud of old paper.

Black and stars and more blackness. Through the fog of near-unconsciousness, there was a feeling of urgency, that I couldn't just lie there and hurt. I rolled over, a motion that hurt almost as much as anything I had ever experienced. Grabbing onto the shelf, I pulled myself up enough to see. The room was dark, the only light coming from the hall behind me. Miika was slumped on the floor, while Nieminen picked himself up from the ruins of another shelf on the other side of his makeshift altar. The table lay on its side, its legs pointed toward me, and I couldn't see Susan.

With a snarl, Isabella launched herself across the room, pages of paper floating about her. Nieminen waved his hand, and she hit an invisible wall, bouncing off and rolling across the floor. He stepped forward to face the cat's threat.

I managed to fight my way to my knees, drew my athame from my bag, and threw it. The knife hit Nieminen in exactly the same place as when I knifed him before, and he screamed.

Isabella sprang at him and knocked him down. The table obscured my vision, but I saw Isabella roll head over heels out from behind it. Nieminen stood and raised his hand with a fireball ready to hurl at the cat.

Struggling to my feet, I waded through paper toward him, thinking, *Is this guy crazy? Has he seen all the paper in this place?*

I thrust my sword into Nieminen's back all the way to the hilt. He stiffened, and the fireball in his hand sputtered, then began to shrink. It winked out, and Nieminen fell forward, sliding off my blade.

Susan O'Shaughnessy screamed. I leaned forward and looked over the table. She hung there, her limbs still pinned to the table.

A small black-haired woman dressed in red walked past me, around the table, and picked up the statue. All three hundred pounds of it. It was almost half her size.

"Thank you," Akari Nakamura said with a smile. She made a motion with her hand, and I found myself frozen in place. "This has been quite an entertaining quest. After setting that tracking spell on your kitty, all I had to do was sit back and let you lead me to it. I had no doubt of your ability to find it. You're so earnest and persistent."

Her eyes turned down to Nieminen and the wailing O'Shaughnessy. "Such hubris. Hubris and stupidity." Her eyes rose to me. "I find the two often go together, don't you agree?"

She started to walk past me to the door. I didn't know if she'd forgotten Isabella, or thought the jaguar was no threat, but she never even glanced in that direction. So, she didn't see the jaguar morph, her form becoming that of a woman in a jaguar skin, her head that of a jaguar with an almost-Human face. Not Isabella's face, but one so terribly beautiful that it almost hurt to look at her.

Ixchel reached out with a long-fingered, fur-covered hand ending in three-inch claws and grabbed Nakamura around the throat. The mage's eyes bulged, her tongue protruded from her mouth, and then she died without a sound. It was shockingly quick. The statue fell to the floor.

The goddess leaned down and picked it up with one hand, then turned to face me. She smiled, revealing fangs that would put a vampire to shame, and dipped her head in a slight nod. With a sideways shuffle step, she parted the veil and disappeared.

I found myself able to move again. Susan O'Shaughnessy continued to whimper and sob. Looking around the room, I was astonished to see Isabella standing there in her Human form.

"You're still here."

"Yes. Mother has never been the maternal type."

Out in the hall, we found Karen and the other agents. All had been frozen like I was, but none of them appeared to be injured. I went back inside and knelt down by Miika. He was barely conscious.

"Silly man. You've exhausted yourself," I said.

"We won?"

"We won."

He closed his eyes and fell asleep with a smile on his face.

Everything went black. When you're in a basement with no light, it is very, very dark. I looked toward the doorway, and even with my Elven sight, all I saw was black.

Not wanting to lose Miika, I straightened him out, then picked him up and carried him toward the door, shuffling my feet and trying not to trip over anything. He weighed about the same as Isabella in her cat shape, but he was much longer. I thought I did well. I didn't drop him and only bumped him into the wall once before I found the doorway.

"Isabella?" I asked as I stepped into the corridor.

There was a little bit of light there. It came from the emergency exit lights set at intervals near the ceiling.

"Yeah," she said. "We lost power."

"Did we do that?"

I heard her chuckle. "Naw, I think Torbert did. At least, I hope he did."

I kindled a mage light and accompanied Patterson's men back into the room where they freed Susan O'Shaughnessy. They carried her and I carried Miika. We found stairs leading up to the first floor.

Karen managed to contact Torbert, who told her the President's speech had been cancelled. Patterson called his superior and reported that we had neutralized the threat. For my part, I was bone tired and thirsty. All I wanted was a glass of water and a place I could lie down.

We came out on the ground floor and sought an exit. That was when we ran into soldiers, who pointed guns at us and ordered us to put our hands in the air. It was an effort doing that while holding Miika, but I managed.

"We got separated from our tour group when the lights went out," Isabella said. "Can you please direct us to the nearest exit?"

The soldiers stared and Patterson laughed. He held up his identification and said, "Patterson, Secret Service."

Karen held up her ID and said, "FBI."

"What are you doing here?" a soldier with little gold birds on his shoulders demanded.

"We work here," Patterson said. "I might ask what the military is doing in a civilian institution. Did you get lost?"

They wrangled back and forth for a while, then

Patterson made a phone call. I sidled closer when he handed the phone to the soldier.

"Colonel, this is Attorney General Mathew Adair. Are you part of this coup d'état some of these generals are attempting? I'm telling you, those who are part of this conspiracy are going to regret today. The President plans to prosecute the traitors to the full extent."

We were soon escorted outside and medical personnel attended to us. About an hour later, several PCU men that I recognized showed up with a couple of cars. One of them offered to take Isabella, Miika, and me home.

I gratefully accepted, but Isabella asked, "Can we stop by a take-out joint on the way? I'm starving."

CHAPTER 29

A week after we saved the U.S. Government from destruction, I threw a dinner party. Torbert, Karen, Miika, and Isabella, along with Tom Edwards and Daniel Patterson, made up the guest list. Although I couldn't get all the proper ingredients, over the years I had found passable substitutes, so I served a true Elven feast.

I hadn't had a dinner party at my house since Carolyn got sick. She used to love to entertain, though she didn't do it often. It was always close friends, almost all of them witches or mages. She used the occasions to show off our culinary skills, fixing fancy dishes that were a lot of time and trouble, dishes we almost never fixed for ourselves.

The damage Nieminen and Bronski had caused was still not solved. The conflict within the military almost led to a civil war before the anti-paranormal Army commanders who took control of DC stood down. Congress was in an uproar, and there was talk of impeaching the President.

Outside DC, the anti-paranormal, anti-witch sentiments that had caused such pain and upheaval two years before had risen back to the surface. Conspiracy theorists refused to believe the paranormals were innocent, and I'd read some truly tortured logic trying to tie the anti-paranormal Human mages and paranormals together. Some places in the South had declared martial law again.

In the aftermath, the government wanted a lot of my time because they had a lot of questions. After I figured out that many of the people I talked to didn't believe the answers, or didn't want to believe the

247

answers, I stopped having time for them. I had a business to run, and I had lost a lot of money while running around chasing the statue. It turned out that saving the world didn't pay very well, and the insurance company didn't want to replace my Honda.

The morning following the dinner party, Isabella said goodbye. She wrapped her arms around me and hugged me. "I'm going to miss you. Come visit me in Colorado."

"I will. I've seen pictures of the aspens in the fall. That's a slow time for me, so I usually travel in the colder months."

I dropped her off at the airport and drove back to the nursery. I was gradually chopping down the pile of paperwork, and my employees were earning a lot of overtime as we ate into the backlog.

One afternoon when I pulled into the compound, I saw a dark green BMW waiting for me.

"Hey, what's up?" I asked as Miika pushed away from where he was leaning against his car.

"Isabella told me that you're a fan of Irish music," he said.

"Yeah, I am. Do you like it?"

"I do. I was wondering if you'd care to have dinner with me Saturday evening, and then go listen to some music?"

I found myself smiling, a feeling that had been rare the past few weeks. "Sure. I'd like that."

"I'll pick you up at your place. About six thirty?"

"Sounds good."

I watched him drive away. It had been a long time since I'd been on a date. I hadn't dated a Human in a couple of decades. I had never dated a halfling, but he was damned good looking, and he was even a hair taller than I was. Whistling an Elven tune, I headed to the office to check my messages.

###

If you enjoyed **_Gods and Demons_**, I hope you will take a few moments to leave a brief review on the site where you purchased your copy. It helps to share your experience with other readers. Potential readers depend on comments from people like you to help guide their purchasing decisions. Thank you for your time!

Get updates on new book releases, promotions, contests and giveaways! Sign up for my newsletter.

Other books by BR Kingsolver

The Chameleon Assassin Series
Chameleon Assassin
Chameleon Uncovered
Chameleon's Challenge
Chameleon's Death Dance

The Telepathic Clans Saga
The Succubus Gift
Succubus Unleashed
Broken Dolls
Succubus Rising
Succubus Ascendant

Other books
I'll Sing for my Dinner
Trust

Short Stories in Anthologies
Here, Kitty Kitty
Bellator

BRKingsolver.com
Facebook
Twitter

Made in the USA
Columbia, SC
30 January 2021

31939205R00141